Universe Destroyers™
World War II

Kurt Weichert

Published by Weichert Media, 2024

Table of Contents

CHAPTER ONE: CAPE GIRARDEAU, MISSOURI

*A*PRIL 12, 1941...

Sweat was pooling at the top of Pastor Timothy Harding's bald head, beneath the cap he had donned when he hurriedly left his home half an hour earlier. Harding had just arrived outside of the Cape Girardeau airport in Missouri. It was April, so it wasn't that hot, but Harding was anxious. He rolled up to a field in his car and saw that the area was swarming with official government personnel: there were firefighters everywhere, police officials—both local city cops and sheriff's deputies—two men in black suits and fedoras with grim looks on their faces, and about a dozen military personnel. Standing before Harding's car, in fact, was a Sheriff's deputy and an armed American G.I. with an M1 Grand rifle. The deputy looked bored, and the young soldier was pale. A makeshift cordon had been erected in a perimeter and a sleek, silver metallic craft looked as though it were welded into the ground.

Harding was nervous because he had received a frantic phone call while in the middle of preparing his sermon for the coming Sunday service at the Campland Baptist Church, where he was a pastor, when the police dispatcher had called on behalf of the Cape Girardeau police chief, Marshall E. Morton. Harding had recently moved to Cape Girardeau and was still getting to know the townspeople and the local leaders. When he had picked up the phone, the dispatcher immediately passed her end of the line over to Chief Morton who had spoken in curt, clipped tone, and commanded Harding to head to a field to the southeast of the local airport. A tragedy had just occurred, Harding was told by a somewhat ambivalent-sounding police chief: a small commuter plane had crashed and there were fatalities who needed spiritual attendance.

As Harding surveyed the scene, though, he realized that this was not an ordinary plane crash. The presence of armed U.S. military personnel was the first tip-off for Harding. *Maybe it was an Army bird?* Harding mused to himself. Annoyed by the sweat pooling under his cap, Harding removed it, pulled a wrinkled handkerchief from the left pocket of his black slacks, and dabbled the sweat away.

"State your business, sir!" The young soldier demanded, firmly gripping the barrel of his rifle, which he had moved from his back to holding it pointed in Harding's general direction.

Harding's face contorted in shock and he spastically raised his hands. The more seasoned Sheriff's deputy placed his right hand over his pistol that was still in its hip holster, and raised his left hand calmly, motioning for the soldier to calm down and lower his rifle. "Relax, kid, he's a local pastor not a Nazi spy."

The G.I. was shaking, though, prompting Harding to wonder if he had even finished Basic Training. Harding couldn't figure out why in the world this G.I. was so tense. America, unlike Europe and Asia, wasn't at war. Sure, FDR had been warning about the threats that Hitler posed the world and was standing up to the bloodletting that Japan's armies were subjecting the poor Chinese to in Nanking, but there was absolutely no reason for a soldier to be this defensive in the middle of the American heartland.

From behind the two guards, Cape Girardeau police chief Walter Morton approached. He was a short, bespectacled man with a stern look upon his pudgy, round face. His round-rimmed glasses had a strange yellowish tint to them, and his teeth were slightly stained from what Harding assumed was years of coffee drinking. "Ah, gentleman, this reverend is with me." Morton said coolly as he got nearer to the guards. The sheriff's deputy glowered at the city police chief but relaxed almost immediately whereas the soldier acted as if the chief wasn't present. The sheriff's deputy moved aside slightly to allow for Morton to pass but the soldier wasn't budging. The chief stuck his stubby right arm forward, extending it into the space between where the sheriff's deputy had stood and where the young Army soldier was standing tensely. Morton waved the apprehensive Harding forward.

Harding locked eyes with the cool Morton and then reached into the backseat of his car and pulled out a worn Bible and his sport coat. He approached the uneasy soldier and weary sheriff's deputy slowly, Morton scooted to the side that the sheriff's deputy was standing on to make way for the scared pastor and allowed for the pastor to come alongside Morton. As Harding passed the worried soldier, he whispered, "Go with God, son," and quickened his pace to be beside Morton, who was clearly unafraid of the spastic soldier.

"There ain't no God out here, Pastor!" The soldier said skittishly.

The pastor stopped and glared back at the young soldier. The soldier, who remained clinging his rifle fearfully looked as though he were possessed by Beezlebub himself. "Yeah, you come talk to me after you see what's back there," the soldier said, replying to the accusatory glance that Harding had shot over at the soldier.

Before the pastor could respond, in an attempt to prevent from what the pastor feared was a young soul falling into the Devil's grip, Morton's powerful right hand grabbed onto the pastor's left shoulder and squeezed momentarily, urging the pastor to move on.

"Peacetime Army." Morton muttered wryly.

They began walking toward the downed craft that was standing on its side, crashed into the ground, on an angle. At first, Harding reasoned that it was a wing. But it was massive wing meaning that the aircraft that crashed here must have been gigantic. It certainly could not have taken off from the local airport, as Harding had been told over the phone by the chief.

"You settling in nicely?" Morton asked gruffly, surveying the activity that was bustling around them as they followed what appeared to be a well-worn path that led directly to the underside of the strange, downed craft. Smoke bellowed from the field, the closer they got to the craft.

Harding was silently gripping onto his Bible. There was something extraordinary happening here today—and he was dead in the middle of it.

"Pastor?" Morton prompted coolly, clearly trying to keep the confused clergyman's mind off what was transpiring; keeping him focused on putting one foot ahead of the next, so Morton could wrap this event up, and get these military guys out of his town.

"Y-yes. Thank you." Harding said, staring as he watched four soldiers carry a long wooden crate from the opposite side of the downed vehicle and load it into a flatbed truck. Standing beside the downed aircraft were the two G-Men in black suits and black hats. They stared unblinkingly at Harding as he approached the craft. Harding and his police escort rounded a mound of dirt, rock, and dry grass that had been kicked up by the crash, where the entire field in front of them that led to the base of the crashed vehicle was strewn with what appeared to be thin, rumpled sheets of metal that looked more like tinfoil from his kitchen than it did parts of an airplane. Harding started coughing as he inhaled smoke that became increasingly thicker the closer to the downed craft he and Morton got.

Morton had already placed a red handkerchief over his mouth, to better protect his lungs from the smoke. Seeing the chief of police do that prompted Huffman to place his own white handkerchief over his mouth as he started to instinctively cough from breathing in the smoke. The closer he looked at the crash site through the thick smoke, the more Harding could see that there were embers across the field—emanating from the countless bits of various-sized tinfoil-like metal debris strewn about the place. Firefighters were standing and spraying water on the different burning pieces of debris, clearly concerned that the field could catch afire.

"Well, pastor, the community is just so glad to have you with us at the Campland Baptist Church." Morton said reassuringly, trying not to feed into Harding's sense of amazement at the crash site arrayed before them.

Harding looked away from Chief Morton and stared at what appeared to be an opening on the underside of the craft that, now that Harding was within spitting distance of the crashed vehicle, he could tell that this was no ordinary airplane. It was a saucer of some kind. The bottom had been opened and three men in US Army officer's uniforms were inside the craft, talking amongst themselves; they were inspecting the vehicle and touching various panels—as though they were trying to see how the thing worked. None of the official personnel in the field seemed particularly concerned about the raging fires all around them.

To the right side of the opening of the slanted saucer that was firmly nestled in the field on its side, sticking straight into the air, were two soldiers posing for another soldier holding a large, clunky camera. The two soldiers held the most shocking thing that Harding had ever seen in his life: a short, grayish being—no more than four feet tall, almost childlike but strangely different—with slits for a mouth, two black dots for a nose, the tiny creature was totally hairless, too. It had two huge eyes with vertical slits for pupils. Its arms were extraordinarily long, with three elongated fingers, and the whole being appeared to be made almost of rubber. In fact, Harding's last place of refuge in his mind was a comforting—though somewhat unbelievable— thought that perhaps these were dummies of some kind, since the flesh and the way the soldiers were moving its limbs appeared rubbery and bouncy, like a dummy.

The two soldiers were laughing wildly as they lifted the strange being, each soldier with their arms underneath the two arms of the being, holding the gray creature up before the camera and smiling wildly. After what seemed like an eternity, the camera flashed, making a loud *pop!* as it snapped the incredible black-and-white photo. In that moment, the Army photographer, who was also grinning widely, peered from behind his camera and said jokingly, "That's one for the history books, fellas!" Harding thought that the scene was more reminiscent of a successful hunt of a strange, exotic beast rather than an emergency medical response to a plane crash.

Buckling under the weight of the alien being, the two soldiers lost their grip on it and dropped the creature roughly to the ground. The photographer grimaced at the sight of the two soldiers manhandling their prize. The two young soldiers laughed even harder as they saw the tiny being they had held up for the photo crash to the ground and bounce up for a moment before crumbling on its side, as though it were a deflated balloon.

Momentary rage flashed over Harding as he believed he had just witnessed the carefree G.I.s disrespect a victim of this strange, horrific crash. For all they knew these could be the mutilated bodies of young children who were onboard whatever kind of airplane this was, and there these two soldiers were holding one of those victims up like they were a buck shot on a hunt. One of the Army officers who had been inspecting exposed interior of the craft behind the two loopy soldiers had glanced out from the craft and saw Harding standing beside Chief Morton with a mortified look upon his face. The Army officer moved swiftly outside of the crashed craft and positioned himself directly over the two soldiers who were kneeling, inspecting the strange being. The Army officer, who had the gold bars of a second lieutenant on his shoulders, pointed at the two, giggling soldiers.

"Now you two men knock it off!" The second lieutenant commanded.

The two young soldiers nodded slowly, a look of madness momentarily in their eyes. They stared up at their commanding officer. The one closest to the downed creature composed himself and nodded. *"Yes, sir."* He whispered.

Morton tugged on Harding's left arm. "Put your coat on, Reverend." He said calmly.

Harding, who had forgotten he had brought his sports jacket along with him, glanced down and saw the jacket dangling from his left arm. He shot a quizzical look at Morton. As if reading Harding's mind, Morton pointed at the three tiny bodies lying on the field before the downed craft and said, "There are your victims. You've got to administer their last rites."

Harding recoiled. "I'm not a Catholic priest. We don't do last rites."

Morton chortled. "Just pray over them, please. Some of the guys out here are very jittery—"

Harding nodded. "I can see that." He muttered. And then, after he finished putting on his coat, he glared firmly at Morton. "So am I, by the way."

Morton shrugged. "It's important for the sake of everyone here that we maintain some semblance of normalcy." He directed, his tone moving from calm and ambivalent to officious.

Harding glanced at Morton with a look of concern. Morton, who was clearly troubled by what was transpiring, sighed loudly and took on a brief apologetic face. "Or at least that's what the feds tell me..." Morton added in a conciliatory tone. Harding glanced back at the officer who was standing over the bodies. The two soldiers he had reprimanded had walked off to the other side of the crash site, their rifles slung around their shoulders.

The second lieutenant then turned to face Harding and Morton and motioned for them to approach the bodies. Morton nodded and started walking toward the second lieutenant. Harding's eyes widened and he suddenly was overcome with apprehension to the point that he was unsure if he could move. As if guided by the Holy Spirit itself, despite his fear and anxiety, Harding did as he was commanded. When he arrived standing directly over the three tiny bodies, he knew that these were not disfigured children. These were beings from elsewhere. His heart began racing. Harding pushed away the internal screaming that was resonating throughout his mind; he resisted the urge to turn tail and flee back to his car and flee this evil place. Rather than give into his fear, though, he clung harder to his Bible.

He said a prayer in his mind and kept staring at the little people laid before him. After reciting the prayer in his head, he was calm. Empathy and compassion swept over him as he realized that these beings—whoever or whatever they were and wherever they were from—must have had a rough, painful last few moments on this planet. That fact anchored the scared pastor and allowed for him to fall back on his training. He knelt beside the being that the soldiers had roughly handled and taken their photograph with.

"This is Pastor Timothy Harding of the Campland Baptist Church." Morton said, waving over Harding.

The second lieutenant's face contorted, and he repeated, *Campland?* "You're not a Baptist are you, lieutenant?" Harding inquired. "Methodist." Harding, doing his best to ignore the fear of the situation unfolding around him, and desiring to glam onto anything familiar, decided to minister to the young Army officer. He raised his Bible slightly and with his free hand and began preaching, "The third angel blew his trumpet, and a great star fell from Heaven, blazing like a torch, and it fell on a third of the rivers and on the springs of water." Overcome with what Harding believed was the Spirit, he pointed at the downed craft and the burning field with his free, right hand and proclaimed, "The name of the star is Wormwood. A third of the waters became wormwood, and many died from the water, because it was made bitter. Revelations eight, ten-to-eleven." Harding concluded solemnly.

Harding's words were a bit too loud, some of the soldiers had moved toward where Harding was standing over the dead bodies of the occupants of the downed craft, and the second lieutenant glared angrily at Harding. Morton, seeing the crowd form, smiled calmly at the handful of troubled soldiers and put his hands up as if motioning for them to stand down. "All is well here, fellas. The pastor is just giving last rites to our friends over here."

A wiry, blonde-haired soldier who looked like he was a mere teenager stood beside one of the soldiers that the second lieutenant had dismissed. "See, I told you this here thing was from Hell! The minister is quoting from Revelations!"

"No, no! He's giving last rites." Morton said reassuringly.

The second lieutenant shook his head bitterly and continued staring at what he viewed as the hapless reverend. Another Army officer, wearing two bars on his shoulders, indicating that he was a captain came storming out of the downed craft. "You boys report back to your posts, damn it!"

At seeing their senior officer on the scene, Captain Harold J. Shelden, Jr., the Army soldiers stood at attention and snapped a crisp salute and resolutely dispersed to other points in the field. The captain motioned for the second lieutenant to speed things up.

Morton sighed and shook his head. "Anyway, Pastor Harding, this is Second Lieutenant James E. Lightie." Morton announced.

Harding extended his hand for Lieutenant Lightie to shake but the second lieutenant just shook his head. He looked over angrily at Morton and said sternly, "You see, Chief, this is why I didn't want any unofficial personnel here!"

Morton shrugged sheepishly, being subjected to the same curt treatment that he had subjected Harding to. "I understand that, Lieutenant Lightie, but my guys were very troubled by this whole thing. And clearly so are yours."

"Be quick, please, Reverend." The second lieutenant said brusquely.

Harding nodded, composed himself, and knelt beside the corpses, running his hand along the exposed gray skin of the beings, marveling at how alien they looked. Just as he started to recite a prayer, he saw that the being he was kneeling beside—the same creature that the soldiers had taken a sloppy photograph with—was still breathing! Harding's heart jumped at that, sending him to his feet. "Gentlemen!" He exclaimed, doing his best to control the volume of his voice, realizing how upset even the supposedly trained soldiers and police officers standing around them were, not wanting to evoke their ire.

Lightie grimaced and glared over at Harding with a dismissive look in his eyes. Morton stepped forward and stared at Harding calmly. "What is it, Reverend?"

Harding pointed at the downed being. "This...person is still alive!"

Lightie cocked his left eyebrow quizzically and casually regarded the being below their feet, who was clearly breathing—albeit shallowly. He then looked calmly up at Huffman and said nonchalantly, "No, he's not."

Harding looked back down and pointed at the being's chest. "Yes, lieutenant, he is!" Harding insisted.

Lightie remained staring at the reverend. "It's a dead man's twitch." Harding furrowed his brow in confusion. "Corpses sometimes move after they've been killed." Morton interjected in a calming tone.

Harding looked back down at the corpse who was now leaning slightly up, its wide, vertically slanted eyes staring directly into Harding's, and pointing its straggly, elongated, gray index finger at Harding. Compassion and sadness at the helpless state that this bizarre, tiny being was in—and the callousness of the men who were supposed to act as saviors during the crisis— consumed Harding. Lightie shoved his right index finger aggressively into Harding's chest and insisted, "You don't understand, Reverend: it's a dead-man's twitch!"

Harding looked helplessly over at Morton, who stared sternly at Harding. "Oh, look, it's stopped moving." Morton said calmly. Sure enough, the being had stopped breathing and pointing. Harding noticed Morton's left boot was very near the being's throat. A dark thought crept into his mind: did the police chief silently murder this being while Harding was distracted by Lieutenant Lightie? The cold looks in both Lightie and Morton's faces said everything that needed to be said: if Harding wanted to get out of this situation alive, he'd shut his mouth. Before Harding could act any further, the downed craft began humming loudly; the ground began to shake, and everyone began running about the place with barely contained panic upon their collected faces. Harding instinctively knelt and covered his head, as he assumed the craft was readying to either take off or explode.

Another Army officer, who had lieutenant bars on his shoulders, came running out of the craft screaming, "I didn't touch anything, sir!"

Lightie waved the lieutenant over, who was their medic, First Lieutenant Lucas L. Digiglia "This one just died!"

Harding shook his head, refusing to look up as the ground shook violently.

"Look at the bird!" One of the G.I.s yelled from the background, referring to the downed craft. Gripped by fear and believing he could die at any moment, Harding looked up at the sky to pray one last time. When he did, the pastor was mesmerized by what he saw as strange, glowing writing scrolling along the sleek, silver hull. The writing glowed an orange-red and appeared to Huffman as ancient Egyptian hieroglyphs—though he could not be certain, as he was not an expert in ancient languages. As quickly as the commotion from within the strange craft had begun to rock the area, the loud humming noises ceased, the ground stopped shaking, and the hieroglyphs disappeared.

There was an eerie, long silence that fell over the crash site—save for the crackling of the flames from the tinfoil-like debris strewn about the field and the splashing of water flowing from firehoses. Once everyone felt safe that the craft was not going to explode or launch into the sky, Lightie looked back down at Harding who was recovering from the spectacle. Another bit of commotion erupted from the outer cordon. Harding glanced up and saw a line of massive, green flatbed Army trucks. A crane was in the Army convoy as well.

"We're leaving." Captain Shelden said firmly, walking quickly past Lightie and Morton, toward where the convoy was entering the cordon.

"Yes, sir!" Lightie snapped a salute. "Let's get this place cleaned up!" He ordered the Army personnel assembled.

Harding composed himself, now totally committed to giving these poor beings some semblance of a respectful, Godly sendoff. Harding knelt beside the beings and began administering a prayer to send them on what he had hoped was their way to the Lord.

Harding shook as he quietly prayed over the strange beings, deeply disturbed and scared that these men may have murdered the people here. But Harding dared not say another word.

Clearly, these official men wanted silence. When he finished the quiet prayer, Harding did the sign of the cross in the air above the downed beings and stood up mournfully.

"It's finished." Harding said solemnly, refusing to look at either Morton or Lightie— keeping his gaze transfixed on the dead creatures laid out before him.

"Follow me, Reverend." Morton snapped, helping the reverend to his feet because Harding was simply taking too long. As Morton escorted Harding away from the wreck, the pace of activity intensified as dozens of more soldiers exited the flatbed trucks and began moving toward the crashed craft. The smoke had died down, too, as the firefighters had effectively managed to douse most of the fires that were burning throughout the field.

When they rounded the mound of dirt, grass, and debris that had formed a natural barrier blocking the view of the crash site from the road, Morton pulled the dazed Harding back to his car. There, the soldier from earlier who had denounced God was standing with a knowing look upon his face. Leaning against the reverend's white Studebaker was one of the black suit-and-tie- wearing FBI agents. He was tall and pale with piercing blue eyes. The agent wore a black fedora as well and his Bureau-issued pistol hung lazily in his chest holster, which made a hollow clicking sound from behind the agent's black jacket as he approached Morton and the disheveled Harding. The agent also had thick, jet-black hair beneath his similarly colored fedora, which had been tilted slightly to the right.

Harding girded himself against what he feared might have been an attack from the stone- faced, pale agent. In fact, as Harding approached the agent, the G-Man had reached slowly— menacingly—into his right breast jacket pocket and moved his hand around, as though he were covertly unholstering his gun. Harding said a prayer of forgiveness to himself, expecting the worst. Morton looked away, as though he were about to be an accomplice to something dark and terrible.

Harding was now standing face-to-face with the creepy agent. The agent remained staring coldly at Harding and then flashed a Cheshire cat-like grin at Harding; as though the agent had found whatever it was he was scavenging in his right breast pocket for. He brought it out. Harding winced, expecting the agent to reveal a gun. Instead, the agent pulled out a pack of cigarettes and a lighter. He motioned for Harding to take one. Harding regarded the cigarette suspiciously for a moment, he'd never been this fearful of authority figures in his life. He shook his head. The agent shrugged and placed a stogie in his own mouth, lighting it up. When the agent flicked the lighter to its fiery life, Harding jumped slightly.

"Why're you so damned jumpy, Reverend?" The agent asked, puffing smoke at the pastor's fearful face.

Harding swallowed hard. "Long day doing the Lord's work, Agent...?" "Greaves." The agent said in between puffs of smoke. "Special Agent Patrick Greaves." Harding nodded. "Pleasure to meet—" *"And this event—none of it—ever happened."* Agent Greaves said ominously. Harding took that cryptic statement in for a moment. He looked over at Chief Morton who was staring intently at Harding. The pastor nodded slowly. "Yes, sir." Morton smiled and placed his hand reassuringly on Harding's back. "It's for our nation's security, Pastor, you understand?" He prompted. Greaves remained staring intently at the pastor. Harding glanced back at Chief Morton and nodded slowly.

"We could be at war any minute, Pastor. The last thing we need is something like this event getting to our enemies..." Greaves

cautioned.

Harding thought about what the two law enforcement officers were saying and, while he was disgusted with his role in this tragic event, Harding couldn't help but to agree with their assessment of the larger picture globally. Hitler's

Germany. Tojo's Japan. Mussolini and his Fascists in Italy. Stalin's communist goons in the Soviet Union...he couldn't but fear that the whole world was closing in around the United States, his beloved country, and Harding worried that whatever he had just witnessed would be the final straw that broke America's back.

"I understand." Harding blurted out, wanting more than anything to get into his car and flee this dark place.

"I need to hear it from you, Pastor." Greaves prompted.

Harding looked confused. He then said, "You've my word, sir, that I'll never utter this to another soul for as long as I live."

Greaves smiled maniacally and then nodded at Morton. *"Good."*

Morton slapped Harding on the back enthusiastically. "Nothing like having the word of a Man of the Cloth!"

Harding looked dyspeptic. "I'd like to go now." He said quietly, his face pale.

Greaves blew another round of smoke in Harding's face and nodded, pivoting on his left heel, spinning around, and walking over to the car door, opening it. Greaves then looked back at Harding and motioned for him to get inside the car. Harding uncomfortably brushed past the demonically grinning Greaves and gingerly entered the car. Greaves slammed the driver's door shut and pointed at Harding through the window, mouthing the words, "Cross my heart and I hope to die."

Harding held the FBI agent's stare for a long while, steeling himself against what was clearly heavy-handed intimidation tactics from the agent, drawing on strength from his faith. He'd done nothing wrong, after all. So, why did he feel so guilty? He shot an accusatory glance over Morton who was looking with concern at Harding through the dirty windshield of the Studebaker. The pastor started the car and slowly backed it up, turning it around toward the road he had entered the crash site through. As he started slowly driving the car away from the bizarre scene, he saw the G.I. who had given him so much grief at the beginning of his strange journey into the unknown and locked eyes with the scared private.

"Did you find God in there, Pastor?" The soldier taunted after the Studebaker as it accelerated away from the grisly scene. Enraged at the incident and by the torturous end the beings had met—possibly at the hands, or boots, of the authorities—Harding hit the gas and sped away, disappearing over the horizon, his thoughts racing as he tried to focus on the road ahead and God.

Greaves continued puffing his cigarette, watching as the reverend sped away, wondering if he was going to have to take more decisive action. He glanced over at Morton whose posture was slightly slouched, revealing a small gut hanging over his police belt and pants. Greaves took another puff of the cigarette. Morton looked over at Greaves.

"He'll be good for it." Morton said reassuringly, referring to the troubled pastor. "We'll see." Greaves cautioned. "Yeah." Morton murmured in reply, removing his police cap, and rubbing his hand through his head.

Greaves flicked his cigarette on the ground and turned to face Morton after the pastor's car disappeared from their view. "And what about your people?"

Morton looked wounded by the question, sensing it was more of an accusation rather than a question. "My boys and I know where our bread is buttered." The chief said sternly.

Greaves scowled. "They're going to keep their damned mouths shut about the survivor?"

Morton looked confused and then remembered the baby-sized gray creature they had recovered from inside the craft that was alive shortly before the pastor had arrived. "I can assure you they've already forgotten about it."

Greaves sighed, calm washing over him. He nodded. "Good." Greaves looked back at the tip of the saucer that was jutting into the air from the ground it had crashed into. The sound of work machines resonated throughout the field. "You know," Greaves began proudly, "I think we might get all this out of here before anyone notices."

Morton nodded. "My boys will see to it."

Greaves nodded, believing the police chief. "No, my men will." He turned around and began walking toward the crash site. Morton remained staring out at the road that the pastor had taken away from the crash site. "Chief Morton," Greaves began.

Morton turned back to face the serious G-Man. "Yes, Agent Greaves?"

"Your application to the FBI Academy has been accepted." Greaves said in a faux congratulatory voice.

Morton grinned from ear-to-ear. "Well, hot-diggity—"

"Congratulations." Greaves said calmly, not letting the police chief complete his celebratory thought. "Now get your people the Hell out of our crash site." He said firmly. Morton scowled and shook his head. Greaves stood staring at the slightly overweight police chief, hoping that he'd hurl an insult his way. Much to Greaves' sadness, the local cop took the insult and nodded. "Consider it done, Agent Greaves." Morton then placed his right index finger and thumb in his mouth and let out a wail of a whistle that resonated throughout the field. Like dogs responding to their master, the Cape Girardeau cops came hustling over to where Morton was standing. *"Pack it up, boys, we're outta here!"*

A PRIL 15, 1941, 12:41 PM, EAST COAST TIME...

"Incredible!" Crackled the voice of President Franklin D. Roosevelt, who sat at his handsome desk made entirely of light-colored Maple wood from Michigan, reading the document that U.S. Army intelligence had compiled on the recent, shocking events in Cape Girardeau, Missouri. The desk that FDR sat at in his cushioned wheelchair was near the windows of the Oval Office in the White House. For security purposes, FDR had kept the shades to the windows which his desk sat before, closed. The world was becoming a scarier place every day. The report that FDR was reading indicated how much scarier things could get. Although, FDR's face oscillated between grim concern and mild amusement, the more he read the document. When he finished reading the extraordinary—almost unbelievable—document, FDR put it down on his desk, removed his reading glasses which were clipped to his nose, and rubbed his eyes in exasperation.

"You boys have had quite the week!" FDR teased the team of his assembled advisers. He picked up the document again from his desk and stared at it for a long moment. "And we're sure this isn't one of Hitler's newfangled machines?" FDR inquired, not sounding convinced of what he was reading.

In the Oval Office sat some of FDR's closest advisers. His dear friend and a man he had relied on throughout his handling of the Great Depression, Secretary of Treasury Henry Morgenthau, Jr., who was situated on one of the two couches that sat across from the president's desk—the couch to FDR's right—and was seated on the edge closest to FDR. Sitting beside Morgenthau on that couch was Secretary of State Cordell Hull. Across from him on the other couch was Secretary of the Navy, Frank Knox, and beside him on that couch was Secretary of War Henry L. Stimson. Standing before FDR's desk was U.S. Army General George C. Marshall. In a chair that he had pulled to the right side of the president's desk, so that he could be closest to FDR, sat FDR's most-trusted adviser and confidant, his former secretary of commerce who was afflicted with cancer, Harry L. Hopkins.

Hopkins was basically treated as a family member by the president. Until he had been diagnosed with stomach cancer a few years before, many assumed that FDR was grooming

Hopkins to be his successor. But, once Hopkins was diagnosed and the disease began ravaging his body, FDR had decided to run again for an unprecedented third term, and FDR kept Hopkins extraordinarily close. Hopkins became a workhorse for the president. Whereas during his days as secretary of commerce, Hopkins was fixated on the Great Depression and enacting the president's New Deal programs, since leaving that position, FDR had moved Hopkins to representing him in foreign affairs.

A year ago, in 1940, after Hopkins and FDR had spent an evening discussing the Nazi invasion of the Netherlands and the end of the so-called "Phoney War," FDR and his wife, Eleanor, had invited a tired (and slowly dying) Hopkins to stay the night at the White House. Since that night, however, Hopkins had never slept anywhere else. He had become a permanent resident at 1600 Pennsylvania Avenue.

Hopkins was a tall man who originally hailed from Sioux City, Iowa. He dressed in well- made, tailored suits and kept his thinning hairline combed to the side. Today he wore a brown, three-piece suit, with a red tie. General Marshall, standing before both FDR and Hopkins, couldn't help but to think Hopkins looked like a tired academic. Hopkins had, after all, graduated *cum laude* from Grinnell College in 1912; the man was an intellectual force and true believer in what many critics had referred to as FDR's "socialist" policies. For FDR, though, he had maintained that he only supported policies that would save America and did not care how they were described. Hopkins loved his boss and mentor. But Hopkins was an ideologue at heart. Like so many men in politics, he had his own agenda.

"This is not one of Hitler's experiments, Mr. President." Hopkins said in his dry, calm Midwestern accent.

FDR shot his old friend a playful look. "Oh?"

General Marshall shook his head and explained, "The craft does not belong to any known nations."

FDR moved his incredulous gaze away from Hopkins and looked up at his stoic, white- haired general. "To which unknown nation does this vehicle belong to, General?"

"Mr. President, this craft and its occupants aren't from around here." Marshal said firmly. FDR's eyes widened. "Where from, then?" At that point, Secretary of War Stimson looked over at FDR, his hair parted down the middle and of a dark gray color with white tips, giving him the look of an elder statesman (which, of course, he was), leaned forward and waved his right hand to get FDR's attention. "They're from a distant part of our galaxy." Stimson said in his mid-Atlantic accent, his voice cracking in the middle of what he knew sounded like an absurd statement—especially a statement made in the Oval Office of the White House.

FDR stared at his secretary of war. "Gentlemen, I know these are trying times," FDR began. "But it is best that we not succumb—"

Stimson stood. Like Hopkins, he wore a three-piece suit. Although his was a sleek gray color with a black tie and a crisp white shirt. It made him look more like a Wall Street banker than a government official. While Stimson had served in multiple presidential administrations, going back to Republican Theodore Roosevelt, Stimson had made his money as a Wall Street attorney—and his style never changed from that profession. "Mr. President, this information comes from a primary source." Stimson said defensively.

"What does that mean?" FDR asked with a confused look upon his face. "You've spoken with one of these...little people?" He asked incredulously, referring to the bizarre report that the US Army had compiled on the Cape Girardeau incident, and glanced over at Hopkins who had looked back at FDR unblinkingly, indicating his seriousness.

"Mr. President, Henry has one of them in his custody." Hopkins said. FDR's eyes widened. "That wasn't in the report." Stimson nodded. "Sir, my people and I were of the mind that we should keep that particular detail out of any printed material for now." FDR nodded slowly, taking in the shocking news. "Yes, I'd say so. Wouldn't want anyone in the press getting a hold of that document, thinking that we're all mad as hatters up here!" He quipped sarcastically. In fact, FDR's jokes hid a deep discomfort with what was being discussed.

Hopkins glanced at Marshal who remained standing quietly.

"Mr. President, we've recently moved the being to a secure location, given the security concerns of late." Marshal said cryptically.

FDR nodded once. "That's a reasonable precaution." "They've moved him here." Hopkins murmured to FDR. FDR's eyes widened once more and he pursed his lips, trying to hold back his emotions.

"What?!" FDR demanded. "I had my soldiers place the being in the bunker under the White House yesterday."

Stimson said matter-of-factly. FDR chuckled uncomfortably. "This is a joke, yes? You're playing a prank on your president." No one laughed. No one even cracked a smile. FDR surveyed the faces of the men assembled around him, trying to gauge if they were, in fact, pulling his leg. He grimaced when he realized everyone was serious. "What are you all talking about?!" FDR demanded. "For goodness sake, the world is burning and you're all playing some kind of intricate prank on me!" He said angrily.

Hopkins shook his head and looked away. FDR's closest friend and adviser had recommended to Marshal and Stimson that they not waste FDR's time with this sensationalism. It wasn't that Hopkins doubted the report. In fact, Hopkins had seen the evidence himself the previous night. Hopkins had other priorities—and as it happened, other loyalties that he believed transcended either his personal loyalty and affection for FDR or to his country. This issue would distract the American president at a crucial moment and Hopkins needs his boss to have his complete attention on the crises at hand, not on some theoretical crisis in the sky.

Henry Morgenthau, FDR's old neighbor from upstate New York-turned-secretary of treasury, looked directly at the president. Like FDR, he appeared to be in a state of disbelief. Bald, with a pointed nose, and piercing eyes that were close together, and pursing his lips, FDR thought Morgenthau looked more like an angry Bald Eagle in this instance than anything else. "Let's go see this visitor downstairs, then, Henry." Morgenthau goaded Stimson.

Stimson furrowed his brow and looked over at Morgenthau. Before Stimson could say anything, Hopkins motioned for the two men to stop talking, but it was Marshal who looked apoplectic. "Absolutely not, Secretary Morgenthau!" He said sternly. "We moved the being downstairs as a last resort and temporarily! Once Fort Hunt can be fully refurbished, then my people will keep the visitor up there under our close supervision." Marshal explained.

FDR leaned back in his wheelchair, taking in the situation. "We can't expose the president to a being like this." Stimson said, backing up his general.

"Well, why not?" Morgenthau asked innocently. "He's downstairs. It's not like you haven't already put the president—this whole building—in jeopardy!" He concluded.

"It's not the same as putting the president directly in front of the thing." Stimson said. "And as the general said, we expect to have a specialized facility built by next week up the road at Fort Hunt." Stimson explained.

Morgenthau shrugged and looked back at FDR. "I agree with Henry." FDR said ruefully. Both Henry Morgenthau and Henry Stimson exchanged bewildered glances. At which,

FDR chuckled. He pointed at Morgenthau. "My old neighbor, Henry. The one man who helped to save this country from the Great Depression." FDR concluded.

Morgenthau smiled as Stimson lowered his head.

"Don't look so down, Henry." FDR said, referring to his secretary of war, Henry Stimson. "I understand what you're saying, too."

Stimson nodded.

"But, since the little man is already downstairs, I ought to be able to see it for myself." FDR insisted. The president glanced back at Hopkins, who was staring down at the edge of FDR's desk. "Harry, what do you say?"

Hopkins glanced up at the president and smiled wryly. "I think you're the president, sir, and it's your house."

FDR beamed. *"Ataboy!"* He said excitedly, appearing to Hopkins as a kid in a candy store, celebrating the fact that his reluctant mother just assented to purchasing his favorite sweet treat.

Hopkins smiled at his boss, but his mind raced. This was a bad idea, he believed. Not only was he concerned that this would possibly compromise FDR. But Hopkins did not want the sentimental FDR to form an attachment with the tiny being that might prevent the creature's transfer from the White House basement to a more secure location. Plus, to Hopkins, this was a distraction. More importantly, given the technology that the Army had obtained from the alien vehicle, Hopkins worried that the US government may be able to leave the other countries of the world behind. Specifically, the Soviet Union.

Hopkins wanted to prevent the reverse-engineering of the alien technology—let alone some new alliance between FDR and another world—to ensure that Washington would be forced to work alongside the communist government rather than dominate it. Hopkins contemplated how best to manipulate the situation to his advantage—and the advantage of his friends in Moscow. Hopkins, like so many of his generation, was a socialist at heart and he wanted badly for his country to evolve into an efficient and egalitarian entity...and it could only do that if it cooperated with other socialist states, like Stalin's Soviet Union, rather than seek to dominate it with superior technology.

The elevator groaned to a halt as President Roosevelt and his closest advisers entered the underground bunker situated directly below the White House. The air was cold and stale. There was a mild buzzing from the lights in the cement corridor; the walls were painted a drab greenish gray. The facility was designed on-the-fly, in response to the sudden and growing threats the United States faced in recent years from the world's vicious tyrants. When the elevator reached the bottom of the shaft and the doors parted, FDR looked up at his weary advisers and he smiled. "Well, gentlemen, let's go meet some faces." He said jokingly and motioned for his African- American butler, Alonzo Fields, who was standing behind FDR's wheelchair, to begin pushing him forward, deeper into the tiny White House presidential bunker.

General Marshal led them down the corridor. The lights gave off a yellowish hue that reflected off the drab colored walls. The air in the bunker made a whistling sound as forced heat blew its way through the confined space. A sense of foreboding filled FDR and some of the other presidential advisers who had not yet seen the creature, such as Morgenthau. Army guards were posted at the four doorways that lined the hallway. One doorway led to a series of rooms with bunk beds. Another doorway led to the room where the loud generators were housed. Still another doorway led to a large concrete alcove where there was a radio and map room. Lastly a fourth door, which lay at the opposite end of the cramped hallway where they were walking, was where General Marshal was leading the men to.

"I feel not unlike Robert Armstrong about to encounter the strange and malevolent beast from *King Kong!*" FDR teased, referring to the popular 1936 monster movie.

"That film did not end very well, if memory serves, Mr. President." Morgenthau quipped from the back of the pack.

FDR laughed loudly, his bellowing laughter echoing throughout the sparsely populated presidential bunker. From ahead of him, General Marshal, unmoved by the conversation behind him (partly because he had never paid much attention to film), glanced back at the president.

"Sir, I'd advise we make no sudden movements or loud noises upon viewing the entity." Marshal cautioned.

FDR nodded. "Of course, General." He said cheerfully.

Harry Hopkins was walking directly behind Alonzo Fields, who was pushing FDR's wheelchair. Alonzo was a rare man. He had served in the White House under FDR's much maligned Republican predecessor, Herbert Hoover, but he was totally trusted by the former president. And, despite the fact that Alonzo would never divulge any information about his former boss, President Hoover, he was as committed and loyal to FDR as he was to Hoover. FDR implicitly trusted Alonzo and Alonzo did whatever needed to be done to help the president, who had been stricken with debilitating complications from exposure to Polio years earlier, without any reservation or complaint. Alonzo and FDR had an unshakeable bond. Any other White House worker would have been forbidden from venturing down to the bunker to see this alien specimen that had been temporarily placed there by the Army. But, when FDR insisted that he see the creature for himself, no one even thought to question the soundness of having Alonzo down there with them.

Hopkins tapped Alonzo on the shoulder. "Alonzo?" Hopkins whispered.

Alonzo nodded and kept his head facing forward, pushing the president's wheelchair, making sure to keep a comfortable distance between FDR and General Marshal. "Yes, Mr. Hopkins?" Alonzo asked politely.

"I want you to keep an eye on the president for the next few days." Hopkins said cryptically.

Alonzo smiled, hiding his confusion by that statement. "Mr. Hopkins, I look after the president *every day,* sir." He replied.

Hopkins nodded sheepishly. "Yes, of course. And, Alonzo, you are wonderful. But we know next to nothing about this creature. Just by being near it could have implications for the president's health." Hopkins explained.

Alonzo nodded. "We understand each other?" Hopkins prompted. Alonzo nodded again. "To be honest, Mr. Hopkins, I'm a little worried about what this thing might do to all of us…" Hopkins recoiled at that. He'd not even thought about the implications to either himself or his other companions about being so near to an unknown being. Yet another reason why Hopkins was opposed to this presidential visit with an alien creature. Before Hopkins could reply, Marshal stopped in front of the green steel door at the end of the hall. A soldier standing guard saluted him. Marshal returned the salute. He then turned to face the group, feeling more like a surly docent at a museum rather than the country's most powerful general.

"The lights have been dimmed inside to accommodate the creature. I would ask that you gentleman stay near the threshold of the door while I take the president inside the room. Remain along the perimeter of the room in the event the creature becomes hostile." Marshal decreed.

Marshal then signaled with his right hand for the soldier standing guard at the door to open the steel door. The soldier nodded in understanding and moved forward, grabbing a green metal handle and slid the door open. It made a metallic whine that echoed briefly throughout the cement bunker. When he finished opening the door, Marshal moved close to FDR and reached for the handles on his wheelchair. Alonzo, who was protective over FDR, consented to being momentarily relieved from his duties of taking care of the president. Without another word,

Marshal began wheeling the thirty-second president of the United States to meet a visitor from another world.

When FDR and Marshal entered the darkened room, which was dimly lit by a single yellowish light from above, FDR instantly felt as though the room were warmer than the rest of the bunker. He removed the blanket that was routinely draped over his paralyzed legs. Marshal noticed this movement and silently reached down and took the blanket from his president, draping it over the handlebars. "We keep this room warmer than the rest of the facility because the creature is comfortable in higher heat." Marshal whispered to the president.

The president nodded slowly, mouthing the words, "Ah," in understanding. He looked around the spartan room. He noticed that there was a single bed with a white pillow, white sheets, and a gray blanket emblazoned with a white presidential seal on the bottom of it, but no creature. FDR's heart beat quickened as he scanned the darkened room, unable to get a good view of much of anything other than the bed. He reached into his breast pocket and pulled out his glasses, placing them atop his nose, hoping that might help. No luck. FDR was reminded of visiting the New York Zoo as a young boy, hoping to see one of the Lions and being disappointed as it was hiding in its pen.

He was slightly frustrated that he was confined to his wheelchair. While he had come to terms with his affliction, there were choice times when he truly regretted and loathed his condition. This was one such time. Had he been a younger, healthier man as he was before the Polio, he'd have walked into the room and gone searching for the creature until he saw it with his own eyes. Instead, he was relegated to hovering on the outside of a room within his own bunker.

"We have determined that our visitor prefers a darkened environment." Marshal's gravelly voice whispered to FDR. "Our scientists suspect that the alien world where this creature hails from is darker than our own." Marshal explained.

FDR was annoyed and seemed despondent. "Well, they must not have much of a society, General." FDR quipped sardonically.

Marshal looked down at the president with a quizzical look.

"Not if they can't see each other or their environment!" FDR joked uncomfortably, referring to the darkened room.

Marshal smiled wryly at that comment.

Will you look at that! Morgenthau's voice exclaimed in what Morgenthau thought was a whisper but General Marshal did not. He shot an angry glance back at the treasury secretary. Now FDR was excited. From beneath the darkened bed before them were two shining, tiny vertical slanted eyes. FDR's face went pale at the sight. He felt as though he were back in Florida, touring one of the swamps near sundown, seeing the eyes of the crocodiles floating in the water shining in the dark. It was both beautiful and terrifying. FDR smiled. He was apprehensive but he did not feel frightened. He was more curious than anything else.

Marshal and Hopkins exchanged weary glances.

"We're through the looking glass now, aren't we, General?" FDR murmured as he stared unblinkingly at the creature hiding beneath the bed.

The eyes started moving, indicating that the being was moving away from its hiding spot. The pitter-patter of feet walking along the cement could be heard followed by a slight wheezing of alien breathing.

"It's moving toward the president." Hopkins said calmly, staring at the creature coming toward FDR and Marshal. "I've never seen it come toward us before." He added, his voice betraying an unspoken fear.

Marshal nodded slowly in understanding. He gripped the wheelchair handles and made ready to turn the president around and wheel him to safety. Before he could act on his instinct to flee with the president, though, FDR glanced up angrily at Marshal. "Don't you dare, General." He commanded in a stern voice. "I want to see this thing for myself!" He insisted.

Marshal glowered at his president but then nodded and loosened his grip on the handles. He may have loosened his grip, but he felt extreme tension in this moment. The being was now inches away from FDR's paralyzed left foot. Marshal marveled at the president. In his youth, FDR was known to be brash and arrogant. He had contracted Polio while doing a marathon swim in the river near his home in upstate New York. FDR came across as a man who was fearless. Marshal wondered if, since having been afflicted with his illness, FDR did not on some level have a death wish or that enjoyed being close to the flame. Of course, FDR had exhibited a leadership style that Marshal had never seen before in an American leader in his lifetime. So, Marshal figured that same risk-taking behavior wasn't all bad; it had saved the country from economic ruination.

The creature was now fully visible in the light. It was no more than two feet tall and it was squat. It had a tiny slit for a mouth, two small dots for a nose, and large, black eyeballs with vertical-closing eyelids. Its skin was an off-gray color and it had three fingers on each hand and three tiny toes on each foot. It was draped in a tiny white sheet that the military had fashioned into a sort of bathrobe. FDR was beaming.

"He's just a baby!" FDR shouted instinctively.

When FDR said that, the tiny creature reached forward with his small left arm, grabbed onto the president's shirt—prompting Marshal to move forward in a defensive posture—and the alien creature pulled himself up to the president's chest.

"My God!" Hopkins exclaimed, worrying that the creature was going to attack the president like a feral beast.

FDR was chuckling wildly, like a man playing with a beloved dog or a toddler. He waved Marshal off and instantly grabbed the being and lifted it up, as though it were a small baby. The president stared into its piercing eyes. And smiled. "Well, hello there, little friend!" He said kindly to the creature. "What's your name?" He asked in a child-like tone. He then pointed himself and said, "I'm Franklin." FDR glanced over at the general, who looked as though he were about to kill the being and smirked. "But my friends call 'Mr. President'!" He said in a jocular tone, but that was clearly meant to remind the concerned group assembled behind him that he was, in fact, in charge here.

The tiny gray alien let out a garbled wheeze that sounded almost like a laugh. This prompted FDR to chuckle. "What a thing!" He exclaimed happily, speaking to no one in particular. "You've been through the ringer haven't you, little friend?"

The alien let out a wheezy hoot in response. "You know, I think he's actually trying to talk to me." FDR said Marshal. Marshal looked visibly disturbed. "Yes, sir." Was all that the general could muster in response to the ridiculous events transpiring. "Aren't you, little one?" FDR asked playfully. The tiny alien let out a series of toots and hoots and FDR's smile widened. He shook his head. "Children. They're the same anywhere, General!"

Marshal nodded. "Yes, sir." He replied coolly, still tense, still prepared to kill the creature if it dared to threaten the president.

"Mr. President, I-I think you might want to put the creature down." Hopkins cautioned. FDR grimaced. "Oh, it's a baby, Harry. Don't be such a wet blanket!" Hopkins shook his head. "Sir our reports indicate that his species is small in stature. The ones that died in the crash measured no taller than four feet." FDR nodded. "And this guy is no more than two feet. So, even for his species, he's a kid!" FDR started making a funny face at the creature, prompting the creature to let out an alien chortle. "Harry, I've been a politician my whole life—made it to the Big House," FDR said referring to the White House, "Kissing babies is part of the deal!" He joked.

"Please don't kiss this particular baby, Mr. President!" Hopkins chastised. "Bear cubs can be cute, too. And dangerous, sir." Marshal quipped in a monotone voice. FDR grimaced at Marshal and then returned his gaze to the small alien. "Well, little one, are you a threat?" He teased. More boops and hoots from the being and FDR smiled once more. This time, though,

FDR's gold watch caught the light and reflected in the baby alien's eyes. He immediately stopped chattering in his alien tongue and let out a "Wooo...." The alien reached forward and grabbed onto the president's watch. This prompted FDR to let out a slightly less boisterous chuckle.

"Uh, sir..." Hopkins began. FDR ignored Hopkins. "Well, General, what are we going to do with this thing?" Marshal looked confused. "Sir?"

"It's just a baby." FDR said incredulously. "A very cute little thing." FDR said, looking back playfully at the creature sitting on his lap. "But, I have my doubts that it'd be a worthwhile ambassador between us and wherever he came from."

"We were...planning on studying him in greater detail, sir." Stimson said from behind the president and General Marshal.

"Yes, at this facility you were building up the road at Fort Hunt." FDR said, sounding unimpressed. "What can a baby teach us?" FDR inquired.

"He could help us understand the craft that we captured." Stimson said. FDR rolled his eyes. "Gentlemen, could a baby fly an airplane?" Marshal furrowed his brow. "No, sir, but—" FDR nodded knowingly. "So, I've my doubts that this tyke will do anything other than look cute and eat whatever kind of baby food it eats." "It'll grow, sir." Morgenthau offered from the back of the awestruck group. FDR nodded, playing more with the small creature on his lap. "Yes, it will. But who's going to raise it? Teach it?" Hopkins smirked at FDR's remarks. "I think what the president is saying," Hopkins began, "Is that, with this thing being so young, it's likely to know only that which we teach it." FDR nodded. "Exactly. It'd know more about us than it would of where it came from or how its spacecraft works." A long silence fell over the group of presidential advisers as they tried to anticipate what the president wanted them to do. "So, what should we do with him, sir?" Marshal prompted. FDR shrugged, staring at the alien creature. "Well, whatever you were initially planning to do with him is a fine plan, General. I just wouldn't throw to many resources into this little guy as I doubt that he'll be the key to unlocking the secrets of the universe as some of you clearly believe he will be."

Hopkins nodded approvingly from behind FDR.

FDR stared a while longer at the playful, small alien and smiled at it once more. He then let out a loud sigh and looked up at General Marshal. "Well, George," FDR said, referring to the general by his first name, "Thank you for this lovely little distraction today. I needed that. It's been getting far too tense lately around here for my liking. Sadly, I'll be needing to return upstairs to continue with my schedule today. We've already fallen so far behind schedule, that Missy may actually murder me!" FDR joked, referring to his longtime private secretary, Marguerite Alice "Missy" LeHand.

Hopkins and the rest of the group let out a chuckle at that. FDR went to hand the small being to Marshal. Before anything else could be done, though, the alien had removed the watch from the president's wrist and was now firmly grasping it in his tiny hands. "Well, you're quite the little bandit, aren't you?" The alien remained staring at FDR, gripping the gold watch. FDR let out another uncomfortable chuckle. "All right, little one, you've got it. Now what?" He teased, reaching slowly toward the watch. Seeing the president's hand move toward the watch prompted the alien let out a small hiss. He then pushed himself off the president's lap, and scurried down, scampering toward the darkened underside of the bed, let out what sounded like a devilish chuckle as he disappeared from the president's view.

"Damn it!" FDR muttered.

"I think we should go back upstairs, sir." Marshal said, grabbing the wheelchair handles again.

"What about my favorite watch, General?" FDR inquired.

Marshal had an exasperated look on his face. "Well, sir—"

FDR shook his head. "I don't tolerate theft in my own house, General, even from such a cute thief. We've got to retrieve my watch."

Marshal nodded in understanding and started moving toward the bed. The clanging of metal could be heard from beneath the bed. "Private, I need a flashlight!" Marshal called out to the soldier standing guard outside the room. Within seconds, the soldier came in bearing a large silver flashlight. Marshal pointed it at the darkened underside of the bed. "Shine it under there, Private." The general commanded.

When the private shone the bright light under the bed, they all saw the small alien sitting on the floor with the gold watch completely disassembled before the creature.

"Well, there goes my favorite watch..." FDR muttered sheepishly. "Kids will be kids, I suppose." He quipped, fighting back a bit of frustration that was welling from within him at the sight of his beloved watch being completely torn apart. "I'll tell you what, little one," FDR called out to the small alien who was not paying the slightest attention to the group. "Consider that a parting gift!" FDR then looked behind him and motioned with his head. "Alonzo, get me out of this God-forsaken room, please!"

Alonzo immediately sprang into action, moving past the group of awestruck officials and grabbing the wheelchair. He began to turn the president's wheelchair around and leave when a high-pitched *"NO!"* could be heard from underneath the bed. General Marshal and the private exchanged concerned looks, thinking the alien was going to become hostile.

"General, look!" The private yelled. "What in the—" Marshal started.

"Oh, what is it, General?" FDR asked in annoyed tone. "Turn me around, Alonzo!" Alonzo did as he was instructed and as FDR returned to his previous position, he was amazed to see the small creature was reassembling—at an inhuman speed—the watch. In a matter of second, the watch was completely restored to its previous condition.

"Hoot-hoot." The small alien said in its nasally, childlike voice. He extended the watch in his left hand so that it was beyond the protective overhang of the bed. Marshal knelt and retrieved it from the alien. He stared at the watch and put it to his ear, to hear if it was working. He heard the usual tick-tock of a watch, and then glanced back at the president.

"Give it here." FDR commanded.

Marshal nodded and handed the watch over to the president. He, too, put the watch to his ear and shook it even. The sight of the president shaking the watch caused the alien to let out a slight chuckle. FDR smiled, "Liked that did you, friend?" He teased.

"How'd it do that?" Morgenthau inquired.

"It likely disassembled it to learn how it worked and then reassembled it." Hopkins said coolly.

"That's quite a talent: being able to build a device it has no working knowledge of simply by taking it apart." FDR quipped.

"Imagine what it might do for more sophisticated technology." Stimson prompted.

FDR nodded in understanding. "Indeed, Secretary Stimson!" FDR looked at General Marshal. "We're keeping him." FDR said.

Marshal nodded. "Yes, sir." *"Here."* FDR clarified. Hopkins' eyes widened in shock. "What, sir?"

FDR glanced up at Hopkins. "We've got spies everywhere, Harry, you know that as well as I do. This little guy is going to have a very big target on his back. And if Adolf or Tojo or Mussolini—well..." He trailed jokingly at the mention of Mussolini, prompting the other presidential advisers to let out a universal laugh.

"Or Stalin." Morgenthau added prompting Hopkins to shoot the treasury secretary a dirty look briefly.

FDR nodded. *"...Or Uncle Joe..."* He said, referring to his preferred nickname for the Soviet leader. "...If any of those bastards got their hands on this little one here, it'd be all over for us—and for him." FDR explained confidently. "No, we keep this guy here. Make him comfortable. But he stays put." FDR ordered.

Sensing that this was the end of the discussion, Marshal nodded. "Yes, Mr. President." He said dutifully.

"All right, Alonzo, get me back to Missy." FDR said. As the wheelchair spun around, FDR called behind him, "See you around, Bandit!"

The men exited the room, leaving behind a smiling small alien. The guard closed the door to the room slowly and FDR could be heard issuing orders to his ministers about what they next needed to do to ensure that the alien's talents could be fully exploited and the secrets of his strange people could be learned before their enemies learned them. FDR, the ultimate organizer, was already pontificating on how his government would create the necessary apparatus for exploiting this strange and amazing being and the technology he had delivered to the unsuspecting Americans.

"Mayor, we need to meet." Harry Hopkins said into the telephone receiver in his private room on the second floor of the White House. He could not believe how the situation with the creature had gotten away from him. The international socialist revolution was at risk, and he suspected that even his Soviet handlers did not realize how dangerous the situation was.

"No, no, no Agent 19, that is not a good idea!" Said Hopkins' Soviet handler, whom he knew only by the codename of "Mayor." While his Soviet handler knew who he was, the handler would never dare utter Hopkins' real name on an open line. *"Where are you calling me from?"* Mayor asked suspiciously.

"My home." Hopkins said cryptically, realizing that his handler was about to blow a gasket. Of course, Hopkins' home these days was the White House, where phone calls were monitored as a matter of course.

The phone went dead. A dial tone quickly replaced Mayor's concerned voice. Hopkins didn't have time for these pedantic games. He quickly hung up the phone. Then, he picked up the receiver yet again and began dialing the phone number of the Amtorg Trading Corporation, the Soviet Union's trade representation in the United States that was based in New York City. After several rings, someone picked up the other end of the phone.

"Amtorg Trading Corporation how may I direct your call?" Came the melodic voice of a woman.

Hopkins shook his head in frustration, pain from his gut, where the doctors believed his cancer was located, began to bother him. The pain usually began when he was stressed. *I don't have time for these intricate games!* He thought bitterly to himself. Hopkins, like so many idealists of his generation who had come to serve in FDR's administration, did not understand why the great governments of the world, who believed in the power of centralization, could not align their efforts in peace.

Had not Stalin proven with his vast central planning in Moscow that communism worked? That communism was a more egalitarian system than anything in the United States? Hopkins knew that if the Americans were able to monopolize the secrets of this alien technology then his dream of a world united by socialism would be dead. The corporate tycoons and defenders of capitalism would prevent the necessary change from occurring—a change that FDR himself had heralded with his New Deal but that so few by 1941 still welcomed. Much to Hopkins' astonishment, even Morgenthau, FDR's old friend and neighbor, had recently testified to Congress about how much of a failure the New Deal was! And with Hitler, whom Hopkins and FDR had tried desperately to get along with initially, increasingly engaged in unpredictable behavior in Europe, Hopkins feared the great vision he had was at risk.

Hopkins recognized that he couldn't avoid playing these silly spy games. He nodded and steeled himself to the reality that he'd need to play by their rules. "Yes, I'm calling in regards to a grain shipment to Minsk..." He trailed ominously.

"Oh, yes!" The woman said knowingly. "Unfortunately, Mr. Grinke has stepped out for a very important dinner obligation." The woman on the other end said.

"Dinner?" Hopkins repeated incredulously. "It's 2:30 in the afternoon!" He insisted.

"Well...uh..." The woman began. She was clearly not as comfortable as some of her comrades were with lying. He could hear her frantically flipping through some papers on the other end of the line. "...I've been instructed by Mr. Grinke to set up a meeting in Washington later this evening...to...discuss that grain shipment." She said, almost forgetting the lie that had initiated their conversation.

Hopkins rolled his eyes. "I see. May I ask with whom I'm speaking?"

There was another long pause followed by an uncomfortable, "Helen Lowry of the Amtorg Corporation."

Hopkins nodded. "We don't have until this evening." He said sternly, assuming that was as soon as Mayor could arrive in town on the train from New York.

"Oh no!" Lowry said excitely. "Mr. Grinke is in Baltimore. His calls are being routed through our offices in New York." She explained. "He'll be able to meet you within the next hour-and-a-half."

Hopkins nodded. "Indeed."

"Mr. Grinke wanted me to know that you'll be dining with him at Ebbitt's Grill." Helen said matter-of-factly.

Hopkins blinked in astonishment for a long moment. "You want me to meet with him in one of the most public spots in all of Washington?"

There was a long pause. "Sir, Mr. Grinke is well known in the capital city."

Hopkins sighed. He thought about it for a moment. It actually made sense. Since he was affiliated with the Soviet trade mission in the United States, Mayor—operating under the fake name of William Grinke—could believably have a meeting with FDR's former secretary of commerce and it not be considered suspicious. Plus, Hopkins knew that the media in this town wouldn't dare try to embarrass either Hopkins or FDR by publishing photos of FDR's closest confidant meeting with a representative for the Soviet Union outside of official business hours. And none of the owners or employees at Ebbitt's Grill would utter a malign word about this matter either.

A light drizzle had descended on the American capital. The black car that had transported the sickly Hopkins, who had donned a gray trench coat and a brown fedora, deposited him on the sidewalk before the brick Ebbitt's Grill. Founded in 1857, Ebbitt's Grill had become a fixture in Washington, D.C. for the nation's movers-and-shakers. It initially existed as a boarding house where multiple famous American leaders had lived and has since become known as Washington's "first saloon." Beginning with President William McKinley multiple statesmen and famous people have graced Ebbitt's with their patronage. Its original location was demolished, prompting the owners to move it to its current location at 1427 F Street NW, about a ten minute car ride away from the White House.

Hopkins opened the wooden door with a glass pane in the middle of it. A tiny gold bell jingled as he opened the door, letting the workers know that a new patron had entered the restaurant. Hopkins smiled to himself as he saw the walls were festooned—as they always had been—with the heads of deer that had been hunted and killed. The intermittent clanging of silverware and the low murmur of intense conversations punctuated the atmosphere. The place was busy but nowhere near as packed as it would be come around 5 pm, just an hour from when Hopkins had entered the bar. The restaurant itself was not that large. It was long and narrow. A long bar extended along the left wall of the restaurant while a large window overlooking F Street was in the front of the space. Several larger tables were there along the window. Opposite of the long bar were a series of smaller tables with chairs, extending all the way to the back of the restaurant, where Hopkins knew the lavatories and kitchen were located.

When he entered, the older bartender with a gray handlebar mustache locked eyes with him and nodded knowingly. He pointed to the back of the restaurant, indicating that Hopkins' party was waiting for him. Hopkins nodded in thanks and removed his fedora and began walking calmly toward where his Soviet handler was seated. As he walked down the narrow space between the tables and the bar, several patrons at different tables and a few seated at the bar, glanced over at Hopkins, instantly recognizing him as FDR's shadow. Yet, since Washington was a city comfortable with power and intrigue, most of the onlookers did not hold their gaze for but a few seconds, and the returned to their own business, perfectly satisfied that they had seen the great man themselves—and were breathing the same rarefied air as this prestigious, powerful man.

Hopkins sighed as he approached his usual table in the darkened back corner of the restaurant, just across from where the back of the bar was. He hung his hat on one of the golden hat hangars that hovered near the table and removed his jacket. A rather pedestrian looking middle-aged man sat at the table looking sheepishly, sipping on what appeared to be Vodka. The man wore a tweed jacket and a simple white shirt with a gray and green check tie. He had thick black hair that was graying along the sides, rosy cheeks from years of drinking, and thick, bushy eyebrows that looked as though they could cover an animal if the Russian man let the hair get out of control. Hopkins sat across from the man he only knew as "Mayor."

"Thank you for meeting with me on such short notice," Hopkins began. The man looked down at his Vodka and said nothing. "We have a problem." Hopkins said firmly. "You know," the man said in perfect English with only the slightest hint of a Russian accent. "You call me—frantic—telling me the sky is falling..." Mayor trailed, sipping his Vodka. "But, tonight I look around and I do not see the sky falling." Mayor said in an annoyed tone.

Hopkins recoiled. "Are you upset with me?"

At that, Mayor looked up at Hopkins and locked eyes. "Goodness, no!" He shook his head, sipping his Vodka again. "You are..." He trailed. "You are the most important thing to us here in this country." The man who pretended to be someone named William Grimke said, almost with love and certainly with adoration in his voice. As he sipped his Vodka, Mayor looked forlorn. "You are, comrade, the goose that lays the golden egg." Mayor said reassuringly, even cracking a partial smile. "And you've always been so good to us."

Hopkins nodded, unsure of where his handler was going with these comments.

Mayor shrugged. "But you expose us—expose me—like this." He said, motioning to their surroundings.

"I never wanted to meet here." Hopkins said defensively. Mayor waved his hand. "Just know, you take risks for us—" *"Serious risks."* Hopkins said sternly. Mayor nodded knowingly. "And we, take serious risks for you, comrade." Hopkins sat back in his chair. "This isn't about me. Or about us, though." Mayor nodded, finishing his Vodka.

"This is about our shared vision." Hopkins said, the idealism of his youth that had never faded with age bleeding into his words.

"Our revolution." Mayor whispered proudly. Hopkins nodded. A grim look appeared over Mayor's face as Hopkins reached down and retrieved a copy of the document that Stimson and the others had presented to FDR earlier that day. He looked around suspiciously and slid it slowly across the table. Mayor folded his hands and lifted them slightly above the table so that the document and the manila folder it was enclosed inside could be slid directly under his hands. After a long moment, Mayor then slid the document below the table and into his own briefcase. "Is it your health?" Mayor asked with dread in his voice.

Hopkins' stomach pained him, overcome by the stress of recent events. Hopkins shrugged and then shook his head. "That's not what this meeting pertains to." He said, trying to calm his Russian counterpart.

Mayor looked befuddled and he placed his left hand underneath his chin. "What is it, then?"

"There is a visitor staying in the White House." Hopkins said, lowering his voice, scared of being overheard by the other patrons.

Mayor looked perplexed. "Explain, please."

Hopkins grimaced. "There's much in that document in the way of explaining what I'm talking about."

Mayor nodded. "I need more than what you've told me, though, if I am to alert the people you want me to about this supposed threat."

Hopkins bit his lower lip and nodded. "A few days ago, on April 12, something crashed near the regional airport in Cape Girardeau, Missouri. A foreign craft of unknown design."

Mayor stared intently at Hopkins. "Luftwaffe?" Mayor inquired, referring to Hitler's air force.

Hopkins shook his head. "No."

Mayor nodded again, his face an empty slate. He was the ultimate spymaster, taking in information while betraying nothing—not even the slightest emotion.

"There was a survivor that the Army picked up from the crash." Hopkins said, trying to gauge if Mayor understood what he was implying, seeing that he was speaking in code and that English was not his first language.

"Right. What did the survivor say, comrade?" Mayor prompted, thumbing his empty Vodka glass.

"It's not so much what he said as much as what he did and who he did it in front of..." Hopkins trailed, thinking back to the extraordinary meeting he had just witnessed between FDR and the strange being.

Mayor frowned. He raised his thick eyebrows and then shook his head. "And that's why you call me here?" He said with incredulity in his voice. "That's why we have this meeting?"

Hopkins sat back and lowered his head. "Grimke," he began by using the man's fake name, "It was a being not from this world and the craft it arrived in is centuries ahead of our technology, as the report I just gave you details." Hopkins explained, leaning forward, and lowering his voice to an almost inaudible level.

Mayor continued staring at Hopkins. He nodded slowly.

After a long moment, Hopkins shook his head. "Do you understand what I'm saying?" He demanded.

Mayor sniffled for a second and shrugged. "This...is not extraordinary to me." Hopkins was stunned. "Wh-what do you mean?" Mayor shrugged. "Such events have occurred in our country as well." Hopkins was confused. "Like this?"

Mayor shrugged again. "Not with living samples, no. But, yes..."

Hopkins took a moment to process what Mayor was telling him. He realized there was a whole world of secret goings-on that even he, as one of the most powerful men in one of the world's most powerful nations, simply was not privy to. "So, you have access to this technology and biological samples?" Hopkins prompted, trying to figure out if his worries were all for nothing.

Mayor looked around to make sure no one was eavesdropping. He then leaned forward and shook his head. "Nothing useful. Nothing—and no one—intact."

Hopkins began to worry again.

"But our reports indicate that something similar happened in 1936 in the Black Forest near Freiburg, in the Reich," Mayor explained to Hopkins, referring to Nazi Germany. "Our people believe the Nazis have working technology from that incident." He added.

"At least you're allies." Hopkins quipped.

Mayor scoffed. He was one of the few Soviet spies who did not think Stalin's pact with Hitler would last very long. "How long will this last?" He asked rhetorically.

Hopkins stared intently at Mayor. "Well, this is what I wanted to talk to you about—in person."

Mayor nodded. "Go on."

Hopkins inhaled and then proceeded to lay out his plot. "This survivor, we've determined is a child."

Mayor shrugged. "How young?"

Hopkins made a clicking sound with his mouth when he remembered the strange meeting in the White House basement. "Hard to tell. But it's a juvenile."

"What good is a child to us?" Mayor asked skeptically. "What about its craft?" Mayor insisted. "The Nazis have one!" He added.

Hopkins bit his lower lip, not wanting to let his Soviet friend down. He shook his head. "No. It's too big and that'll bring too much pressure down on me from Marshal and Stimson."

Mayor was insistent. "You are the great Harry Hopkins. Shadow president. You've moved heaven and Earth for our revolution so far. You mean you cannot move a simple aircraft from a hangar and over to our meeting spot in Nova Scotia?"

Hopkins was annoyed. "No, friend. That is not possible. It'd raise too many questions that I could not answer well enough to avoid suspicion."

Mayor shrugged.

Hopkins leaned in with a momentary look of fear. "Hoover is on the warpath." Hopkins was referring to the FBI's dogged leader, J. Edgar Hoover—a man who saw communists, Nazis, and mafiosos under every bed and behind every door...and he even occasionally managed to find them!

Mayor looked confused. "You can handle him. You've done so well with that thug up until now."

Hopkins shook his head. "Not if I use my position to move the whole craft out of the country."

Mayor looked down, feeling defeated. "Your people have a craft. The Nazis have a craft. We just have a burned-out forest and some folk tales from villagers." He said sadly.

Hopkins looked up. "You don't have a craft at all?"

Mayor shrugged sheepishly. "It is my understanding that we have bits and pieces of one. The Nazis, and now apparently your people, have them intact." He shook his head and cursed in Russian.

Hopkins smiled. "But you have pieces of one?"

Mayor furrowed his brow in confusion at the sight of Hopkins' grin. "Yes, recovered many years ago, in 1908, if I remember correctly, by the tsar's forces in the Tunguska Forest. But nothing works. There are just pieces of the damned thing. The Nazis have an intact craft!"

Hopkins laughed. Mayor looked offended. Hopkins raised his hand defensively. "No, no, you don't understand." He said, remembering how the tiny being disassembled and rapidly reassembled FDR's watch earlier that day. "This little guy could probably make your craft work."

Mayor was confused. "It is in pieces! There is nothing to repair." Hopkins smiled. "I'm telling you, he's the key." Mayor sat back and thought about what Hopkins was saying. Even if the creature in question could not make the bits and pieces of what had been recovered from the cataclysmic explosion over the Tunguska Forest work, Mayor sensed an opportunity to slow the Americans down in their experimentation with the vehicle. The Yanks were already ahead of the Soviets with their atomic weapons program. There was no way that the Soviet Union could afford to let them get ahead in the development of this next-generation technology.

"You can get this visitor out of the country and over to us?" Mayor prompted.

Hopkins grimaced, thinking about how quickly FDR had taken to the being and how he did not want it to be removed from the White House. "Well, the president certainly took a liking to him today." Hopkins said, waiting for Mayor's reaction.

Mayor did not disappoint. For a brief, rare moment, the Soviet spymaster's face went pale. He quickly regained his composure. "This thing is here, in Washington?"

Hopkins nodded and pointed down, the tip of his index finger tapping the wooden table. "In the White House basement."

Now, Mayor's interest was piqued. "What has your president ordered to be done with this...survivor...?"

Hopkins looked away. "He's to be kept downstairs—at least until better accommodations can be built for him."

Mayor nodded. "Where?"

"The military wants to keep it close by." Hopkins recalled. He smiled wryly at the thought of what he was about to say, "They're worried about spies getting wind of it and trying to kidnap or kill the thing."

Mayor smirked maniacally.

"They're refurbishing the old Civil War fort up the road near where George Washington's Mount Vernon home is located." Hopkins explained. "The Army thinks they can have a facility ready by next week."

Mayor's mind was already plotting.

"The president has taken a liking to the thing, though." Hopkins cautioned. "Treated the damn thing like it was a baby...or a dog..." He trailed, shaking his head in annoyance.

Mayor pursed his lips. "*You* have to change his mind."

Hopkins recoiled.

Mayor nodded as if reinforcing his statement. "It's the only way. We have to get this thing away from your military and that can only be done in transit." He said.

Hopkins was silent as he contemplated how he'd get the president to let go of something he had taken such a strong liking to. "I can do that." He said confidently. After all, Hopkins was actually running the daily operations of this presidency. He could probably do what Mayor wanted him to do. "But you can't attack anything in transit." Hopkins added with a tinge of disgust falling over him. Americans would die. "That's insane!" He insisted.

Mayor looked sternly. "If your government is able to master this technology and we cannot keep up with you Americans—or the Nazis, for that matter—then our revolution is dead in its infancy." It was only with the advent of FDR's administration and the rise of so many Soviet sympathizers into the FDR administration that the Soviet Union had been officially recognized by the US government. Since the outset of the Bolshevik Revolution in 1917, the Americans had been violently opposed to Soviet communism.

In 1918, President Woodrow Wilson had sent US Marines to invade Russia and assist the tsarist forces who were fighting to stop the Bolshevik takeover of Russia in the Russian Civil War. Woodrow Wilson's rabidly anticommunist attorney general, William Palmer, had unleashed his determined anticommunist FBI director, J. Edgar Hoover, to hunt down any suspected communist and arrest and deport them as spies. With FDR and the crisis of capitalism in the Great Depression, however, a new day had dawned. Americans were finally receptive to the promises of communism. Stalin and his cadre in Moscow had dreamed of spreading their revolution to the United States through the large and growing Communist Party of the United States of America (CPUSA). Agents like Hopkins and their handlers, like Mayor, were critical to this covert plan crafted by Moscow. But the key was keeping the American government distracted and preventing them from acquiring sophisticated military capabilities.

Hopkins knew what Mayor was saying was true. "I can move him without anyone suspecting." Hopkins said.

Mayor regarded Hopkins for a moment. "How?"

Hopkins smirked confidently. "The same way I've been helping to offload our uranium to you: by official orders." For several months, Hopkins had been instrumental in helping Mayor, who ran five spy rings in the United States—most of which were designed for stealing America's secrets about their atomic weapons program—to get access to basic materials and research that the Soviets would need for their own atomic weapons program.

"When can this be done by?" Mayor prompted. Hopkins thought about it. "Soon." Mayor smiled. "So, you plan on stealing this thing right from under FDR's nose— without so much as a shot being fired?" He mused aloud. Hopkins nodded. "I can get this done." Mayor bowed his head. "Like I said, comrade, you are the goose that lays the golden egg." Hopkins would get the being out of the White House under the pretense that it was being transferred up the road and then he'd surreptitiously change the shipment order and ensure that it was sent up to Canada, along with this month's shipment of uranium—and that it, along with the uranium—would be transshipped from Canada into the Soviet Union.

They started to gather their belongings but then Mayor put his left hand on Hopkins' right wrist. "Be careful. It isn't only your domestic security services you must fear." Mayor cautioned.

Hopkins shot Mayor a quizzical look.

"The Abwehr group here in Washington," Mayor said, referring to the Nazi intelligence spy ring that was operating on the East Coast of the United States presently, "Is getting increasingly belligerent with us."

Hopkins recoiled. "I thought you people were friends." Mayor rolled his eyes. "A brown shirt and a red shirt are natural enemies, comrade." Hopkins was still confused. All his sources and experience indicated that the Nazi-Soviet Pact was strong. These two socialist movements were slated to reshape all of Eurasia into a worker's paradise.

Mayor pulled Hopkins closer to him and whispered, "Comrade Stalin is blinded by the Fuhrer. He believes they are cut from the same cloth, yes?"

Hopkins nodded. "Well, Hitler's National Socialism and Stalin's 'Socialism in One Country' are remarkably similar." He said in disbelief.

Mayor shrugged indifferently. "A piece of cloth is one color. It cannot be red and brown. It can only be brown or red. At some point one dominates the other. This is from Hitler's own book."

Hopkins thought about what Mayor was telling him. He nodded in understanding. Hopkins was aware of the screed that Hitler had written while in a German prison in the 1920s after he had tried to overthrow the Weimar Republic in the Beer Hall Putsch. In that book, Hitler had explicitly written of his designs for conquering the Soviet Union, murdering its people— dubbing them sub humans—and then repopulating the land with Germans. But Hitler's actions since the start of the war indicated that he was seeking just the opposite. And their recent successful conquest of Poland proved, in Hopkins' mind, that the Red-Brown alliance was sustainable. "Does Comrade Stalin believe this about Hitler?"

Mayor smiled devilishly. "Comrade Stalin...thinks many thoughts. Today, he appears enthralled by the Nazis. His affectation for the Fuhrer, I worry, blinds him." Mayor hypothesized. "Hitler has made very clear his plans for our revolution." He added ominously. "One day soon, I fear, we will wake up to a Nazi attack against which we are unprepared for." Mayor concluded.

Hopkins nodded slowly. "I see." Mayor shook Hopkins' hand. "That is to say, watch your back for the Abwehr, comrade." "Indeed, I shall." Hopkins said reassuringly. The two men parted ways. As they exited the restaurant, the older, surly looking bar tender with his thick, white handlebar mustache was standing near the edge of the bar that was closest to the table where Hopkins was meeting with Mayor. He smirked as he had heard the whole thing. The bar tender looked around to ensure that no one would see his next moves. He glanced up at one of the deer heads that adorned the wall above where Hopkins had met with Mayor. Unbeknownst to them, he had installed a tiny recording device in the slain beast's mouth that was aimed at Hopkins' table.

The bar tender knelt underneath the bar and pulled out a small wooden box that was made to look like the boxes that vintage wine were routinely shipped in. It was stamped with the symbol of Vichy France, the portion of France that the Nazis had occupied since 1940. Inside of that box was an intricate recording device. The bar tender checked to ensure that the equipment was running. He breathed a sigh of relief as it was running and had recorded the entire conversation between Hopkins and Soviet handler. He deactivated the recording and removed a tiny tape of the conversation, placing it in his pocket. The bar tender then walked over to the wall behind him which had a big, black rotary phone hanging on it. He picked up the receiver and began dialing the number for his handler, Nazi Colonel Fritz Joubert Duquesne, where he would urge the legendary Nazi spymaster to make his way to the bar and retrieve the recording.

Fritz Joubert Duquesne was a South African born spy who had initially served as a captain fighting the British in the Second Boer War and, because of his animosity toward Britain, joined the German intelligence service known as Abwehr during the First World War. After the war, Duquesne refused to abandon his animus toward Britain. He stayed involved with German intelligence. He was now serving as a colonel in the Nazi-led Abwehr operating under an alias in the United States and running the largest Nazi spy ring in the country. Duquesne was a legend in international spy circles, as he was renowned for having been "the man who killed Kitchener" by sabotaging the famous British admiral's warship, the HMS *Hampshire,* in 1916 on its way to Russia.

Tonight, Duquesne wore a black trench coat to better protect him from the rain and a black fedora. He wore a dark blue suit with a burgundy tie and white shirt. He was tall and thin—very German looking, large eyes with thin lips and very pale. Duquesne had entered Ebbitt Grill an hour after Harry Hopkins and his Soviet handler, the head of illegal Soviet intelligence spy operations in the United States, Iskhak Akhmerov, had departed. The weary Nazi spy gingerly removed his black fedora and approached the bar, briefly making eye contact with the surly old bartender. The bar tender immediately began to pour Duquesne a thick Bavarian beer and slid it toward the Nazi spy, without saying a word.

Duquesne smirked knowingly as the bartender looked away from Duquesne and began wiping down the edge of the bar with a towel. The legendary Nazi spymaster reached into his black coat and pulled out a coin, flipping it toward the old, grisly bartender with a thick handlebar mustache and said breezily, "For your troubles, friend."

The bar tender stopped and placed his right hand over the coin which had landed in front of him. He pulled the coin toward him and looked up at Duquesne. "The trouble is going to be getting out of town here to visit some relatives in Nova Scotia later this month." The man said cryptically. He was not a German. But the bartender was a dedicated National Socialist who was part of the pro-Nazi American Group 76, which Duquesne had been originally assigned to monitor and assist four years prior by his superiors in Berlin. These American men were fervent Nazis and were more than willing to assist Duquesne—with little questions asked—in whatever he needed.

Duquesne nodded. "Traveling out of the country these days can be such...troubling matters, indeed."

The bartender turned around. "Yep, I don't know how, but maybe a friend will come with me—one that lives nearer to Pennsylvania...?"

Duquesne began walking to the other side of the bar, where there were fewer people. "Perhaps take a different, more scenic route, too?" He suggested.

The bartender shrugged, pouring another drink for another patron at the opposite end of the bar. "That entirely depends on who's driving..."

Duquesne smiled again. "Well, a foreign friend always knows foreign land best."

The bartender turned to face his Nazi handler and glowered. "But which foreigner? I'm no friend of the Russkies. And the Italians, they aren't of any help in this matter."

"I think it'd be better if you traveled with one of our friends from Frieburg." Duquesne said in a flat tone.

The bartender nodded. "Well, like I said, I've got until the end of the month to figure out my plans, friend." The bartender grabbed a coaster for the drink he had just poured. "You enjoy that beer." Without another word, the bar tender turned away from Duquesne and marched resolutely to the opposite side of the bar where another patron was waiting for the drink.

Duquesne guzzled his beer, like he were back in Germany, letting the thick white ale flow into his mouth and flood his body. There were things about his native land and about his adopted home of Germany. The beer was one of those things. But everything Duquesne had done since leaving South Africa and joining with the Germans in the First World War was made to ensure that his people were safer and that those who threatened South Africa—notably the British and, by extension, their allies—were prevented from ever harming his beloved nation again.

As he finished his beer, Duquesne noticed a tiny black device at the bottom of his drink. It was a recording that the bar tender had secretly made of Harry Hopkins and Iskhak Akhmerov. Duquesne looked around suspicious to ensure no one noticed him. Duquesne quickly flipped the beer mug over and dumped the recording device onto the bar in front of him. He then scooped the device into his left palm and deposited it into his breast pocket.

Duquesne donned his black fedora, pivoted, and walked outside. He knew from his coded conversation with the bartender that Hopkins was getting ready to move something big from US military custody to Soviet hands. The Abwehr was keenly aware that Hopkins had been instrumental in helping to move materials and designs for what many Nazi scientists assumed was a superweapon that, if the Americans got their hands on before anyone else, would be devastating for the Nazis and their Soviet allies (although Duquesne knew that even now the Nazi leadership was plotting to betray the Soviets very soon). Nazi scientists assumed that it was an atomic weapon the Americans were building. The Nazis were also building their own atomic weapon, though progress was slower than what many had hoped for. The Abwehr had learned that the Soviets were desperately trying to construct their own device, too, and they were using their sympathizers in the highest levels of the US government to help them by stealing sensitive information and critical components, such as uranium.

Given that Hitler was planning to invade the Soviet Union in a matter of months, Duquesne and his massive spy ring had been instructed to slow the transfer of scientific materiel and schematics from the unsuspecting Americans to the technologically ravenous Soviets. He understood that the bartender had overheard enough of Hopkins and Akhmerov's conversation to know that whatever they were plotting was bigger than their normal shipment and it was slated to be transferred from the United States to the Soviet Union through Canada by the end this month. Duquesne was going to listen to the secret recording his agent in the bar had made and then craft a plan to preferably intercept and, if necessary, destroy that critical shipment from America *before* it could get to the USSR.

J ULY 4, 1941…

Bandit, as he came to be known, sat on the concrete floor of the presidential bunker. Dr. Vannevar Bush, the man who was charged by FDR to run America's secret weapons programs— especially the ongoing atomic bomb program known only as the "Manhattan Project"—stood in the darkened room, wearing a wrinkled lab coat. He'd been at this for hours. While the Manhattan Project had, until a few months ago when the alien arrived in Cape Girardeau, been his most pressing concern, the program to unlock the technological secrets of these aliens had become all-consuming for Bush. In fact, Bush believed that mastering the technology they had retrieved in that field outside the regional airport in Cape Girardeau may be more important than the atomic bomb.

Vannevar Bush stood in the doorway with a clipboard with a few other scientists milling about the holding pen in the presidential bunker. He looked tired. As the man running the newly created Organization of Scientific Research and Development (OSRD), his attention span was pulled in a thousand different directions. He was in a race against time and against other great minds in places like Germany, Japan, and possibly even the Soviet Union to develop weapons to both protect his beloved United States and to dominate the world's autocracies. So much responsibility and such little time. It was amazing that Bush hadn't simply collapsed from the stress.

Arrayed before him and Bandit were a series of disassembled devices. There was a shattered glass mug. Beside that was a broken lamp. Next to that, a busted watch. All these devices were of increasing complexity to see what the alien creature could do and reassemble. After the being proved it could reverse-engineer these devices, Bush would then introduce devices his team had discovered from the downed craft that the tiny alien arrived in. Vannevar Bush had asked—demanded, really—that the being be brought to the laboratory where the alien craft and its components were housed at a secret facility in Lynn, Massachusetts that the US government shared with the General Electric Corporation, doing sophisticated research and development on next-generation technology. FDR had personally denied the request. Ever since Hitler's surprise invasion of the Soviet Union, everyone in Washington seemed to be on the brink of a nervous breakdown. Security concerns abounded. Not even Harry Hopkins, the president's closest friend and confidant, could convince FDR to do as Bush had asked.

Bandit, too, seemed to pick up on Bush and his team's stress. In recent days, the strange, tiny alien had become despondent. His skin had started to change colors. Bush had fretted that his health was in decline. Since there was no one on Earth who understood the strange alien's physiology, there was no proper baseline established for what was considered healthy or unhealthy for his species. They did not even know what his species was called or where they were from in space.

"Go ahead, little one." Bush urged the skittish creature that was simply standing before the disassembled equipment, staring blankly.

Bandit purred like a cat, but even his purring was slower and less melodic than it usually was. Bush stared at the being for a long while, attempting to gauge what was going on with him. After waiting for the alien being to take action, he decided to prompt his subject. Bush got down on one knee beside the being and began talking to it like one would speak to a recalcitrant toddler unwilling to do what their parents had asked.

"You don't want to assemble these neat machines for us?" Bush asked the morose alien. The gray alien shrugged indifferently.

"Well, c'mon, just do it once." Vannevar urged, pointing at the glass.

The tiny alien booped and beeped in what Vannevar assumed was a sad tone. He shook his head. It'd been weeks since the little alien had done anything for them in their experiments. What's more, the creature did not eat. Whereas when he was first captured, he ate a collection of leaves—even some crickets—nothing seemed to satisfy him. Vannevar Bush was not psychiatrist but he sensed that the being was homesick.

"Just do this one time and I'll leave you alone for the day, please." Vannevar pleaded, feeling strange as he did. After all, how often did a scientist talk to lab rats? Of course, this wasn't any lab rat. Unbeknownst to the being—or maybe he was aware and wasn't letting on— Vannevar had the military install some monitoring equipment in the ceiling to determine if there was any form of unseen electric current between the alien being and the objects whenever he reassembled them. The Americans under Vannevar Bush were trying to discover the source of the alien's power; to see if it could be replicated and scaled up, to offer the US military the ability to instantly repair any damaged vehicle in combat.

Vannevar had been down in the White House bunker for days. He'd not slept well and he'd eaten even less—despite the fact that FDR had made the delicious White House food available to Vannevar and his staff for as long as they worked in the bunker. But Vannevar didn't care about food. He didn't care about anything other than his work. He knew what the stakes were in the world; true evil was stalking the planet and threatening everything that he knew and loved. And, despite what the American people thought at the time, that evil was marching closer to their homeland. What's more, Vannevar knew—as did FDR—that the real war between America and these evil actors on the world stage, like Hitler's Germany, was being waged in the shadows over who would develop and control the most sophisticated weapons of war. Vannevar Bush feared that Hitler had a leg up on the Americans, which is why he worked himself so hard. It seemed a cruel irony to Vannevar Bush that he'd be forced to tether his success to such a fickle being.

"C'mon, you, do this one for me. And I'll be out of your hair for the evening..." Vannevar trailed, grimacing as he realized the tiny being before him was totally bald. "Well..."

The creature stared into Vannevar's eyes for a long while and then turned around to face the disassembled things arrayed before them. He seemed taken with the broken glass, as it reflected the dim lights from above. The alien creature let out a sound that made it seem like he was saying, *Oh!* Vannevar grew excited for a moment as he saw the alien's right hand extend toward the disassembled glass. He waited with giddy anticipation as he presumed the pieces would lift from the ground and reassemble into a glass, as the alien had done previously for FDR with his watch. After a moment of giddy anticipation, though, Vannevar frowned as he saw the alien continue reaching for the glass. The alien picked up a sharp glass shard and raised it above his bald, gray head. Vannevar immediately became concerned that the creature would hurt himself—or even attempt to slash at Vannevar.

"All right, put it down!" Vannevar commanded, sounding like a stern father speaking to an unruly child.

Upon hearing Vannevar's tone, the tiny alien frowned and spat at him. Anger welled up from within Vannevar. He resisted the urge to smack the being as one would slap a child. So, he stood up in annoyance and kicked the disassembled pieces of machine away from the being, creating a giant mess heap on the concrete floor of the alien's room in the presidential bunker. Vannevar was immediately ashamed that he behaved as he had. He looked away. The alien let out a *"Huff!"* sound and then scampered to the other side of the room, taking refuge in the darkened corner. Muffled sniffling could be heard, as though the creature were crying.

Immediately, Vannevar's heart sank and he looked sympathetically toward the darkened part of the room where the being had hidden itself. "I'm sorry." He whispered, unsure if the being even understood him.

Before anything else could be said or done, the cheerful whistling of the president could be heard from the other end of the hall. It'd been weeks since the president had made his way downstairs. Vannevar knew that FDR had been busy. The moment the Nazis invaded the Soviet Union, their purported allies, the whole world had seemed to be on the brink of something catastrophic. FDR's priorities were elsewhere. Still, the fact that the being and FDR had shared a bond initially and the promise that the being offered to the Americans, if they could just figure out what made him tick, made Vannevar annoyed that FDR would not have made the research down in the White House bunker more of his priority.

Vannevar glanced over at the darkened part of the room as he heard what sounded like excited hoots emanating from the being. FDR had made an impression on the creature, all right. FDR and Alonzo's shadow preceded them as they entered the dim room.

"Ah, doctor!" FDR said ebulliently. "My God, man, you don't look like you've slept a wink!" He chastised Vannevar. "How long have you been down here?" FDR inquired, a look of concern falling upon his face.

Vannevar shook his head and shrugged. "A few days, sir, maybe longer." He said, unsure of how long he'd been in the windowless bunker.

FDR waved his hand toward the scientist. "When was the last time you ate something, man?"

Vannevar looked away. "I told you not to make this such a priority!" FDR continued. Vannevar looked back FDR, annoyed. "Mr. President, this creature may be the key to both the defense of this country from Hitler and his ultimate defeat by our hands!" FDR glowered skeptically. "What child can do that?" Vannevar Bush's eyes widened at that remark. "This isn't an ordinary child, sir. You've seen what he can do." FDR shrugged. "Yes, and has he done it since I was last here?" Vannevar Bush shook his head. "Not really, Mr. President." He said, a tinge of defeat coming over his voice. FDR grabbed Vannevar's arm reassuringly. "There, there, Dr. Bush. I appreciate your dedication, but you really ought to be focused on your other scientific projects." Vannevar was puzzled. "Mr. President, this thing may be the key to winning the next war!" FDR glowered. "You keep saying that. But all I see over there is a scared and lonely child. That atomic program of yours sounds much more promising, if you ask me." Vannevar smirked. FDR had repeatedly indicated in the past that he had no understanding of what Vannevar and his team of scientists meant when they spoke about the atomic bomb. At one point early in their discussions about the weapon, FDR kept asking how such a small weapon could either be built or used effectively in a war—indicating his belief that the weapon itself was the size of an atom.

FDR eyed the mess in front of him. "What's going on in here anyway, Doctor Bush?"

Vannevar slouched forward and sighed loudly. "Oh, Mr. President, we've gotten nowhere with this being."

FDR nodded. "Yes, I can see that." He said ruefully. "But you've made a fine mess in my bunker, I see." He joked.

Vannevar looked over at FDR. "Perhaps you could assist me, Mr. President?" FDR looked perplexed. "I'm not a scientist, Doctor." Vannevar smiled wryly. "Of course not, sir. But you do have a bond with the being and he's not been the same since the last time you were down here...which was several weeks ago..."

FDR frowned. "Well, Dr. Bush, the Nazis have invaded the Soviet Union and Uncle Joe looks like he's in a real pickle."

Vannevar nodded. "As Nazism marches onward, we will ultimately need an ace-in-the- hole to stop that war machine."

FDR nodded. "Bandit?"

Without another word, the small creature came out from its hiding spot and skittered toward the president's waiting wheelchair. He clamored up the president's leg, and nestled himself on the president's lap. FDR chuckled giddily when the being did that. "Well, hello there, my little Bandit!"

The alien giggled madly while Vannevar looked on in amazement. "You've got to talk to it like it's a person!" FDR chided the cold scientist. Vannevar shrugged. "Of course, Mr. President." FDR pulled out a quarter and smiled. "Now watch my hand..." He began. FDR then proceeded to do a trick. He noticed Vannevar staring at him quizzically. "It's an old trick my kids loved. My father taught it to me when I was a boy..." FDR trailed lifting the quarter and showing it to the tiny alien who was clearly in awe of the shiny coin. He even went to reach for it and FDR moved it away. "Now you see it..." FDR said joyfully and then closed his hand around the quarter. "...Now you don't!" He said and opened his hand again, revealing that the coin was gone. The alien was mesmerized and began chuckling. FDR opened his other hand to show that he wasn't hiding it. He then looked concerned. "What's this?" He asked, feigning surprise as he pulled the quarter from behind his right ear. At that, the little alien began laughing uncontrollably.

"I've never seen him like this." Vannevar quipped.

"I keep telling all of you eggheads that a child is a child, no matter where they're from!" FDR said incredulously.

FDR could see that the alien wanted to get its hands on the coin. "Now, if I give this to you, promise me you won't eat it."

"Gwa-gwa-to-Gwa-Nu!" The little alien said in a nasally tone.

FDR furrowed his brow. "I'll just have to take your word for it, Bandit." He said ruefully. Before he could hand the coin over to the alien, though, the alien started chuckling maniacally and revealed that it was holding the coin in its left hand.

"What in the—" FDR said as looked down at his hand where he had thought the coin had been.

Vannevar's eyes widened. "Telekinesis." He muttered and looked over at the adjacent wall where his team had installed a recording device. "I hope you're all getting this!" Vannevar spoke to the covert recording device.

"Twab-tik-Gwa-Oot!" The small alien wheezed.

FDR stared blankly at the being. "I really wish we could understand what this little guy was saying." FDR muttered. *"Me too. But our linguists can't make heads-or-tails of it, sir."* Vannevar explained.

"Neeb-Neeb, Gwa-Tal!" The small alien continued. He then raised his right hand with the quarter inside of it and clenched his tiny fist around the coin tightly. A sizzling sound could be heard.

"What are you doing?!" FDR demanded in an exasperated tone, feeling the being get warmer as it sat on his lap.

"Oot-Tal-Au-Gwa!" The suddenly boisterous small alien said. He then unclenched his fist, which had steam emanating from it. The quarter had been smelted down into hot, liquid metal. The tiny being slightly raised his left hand and the broken equipment and glass began to rise silently from the ground and hover just before Vannevar Bush, whose eyes were wide and face was pale in shock. *"Ong-Ua-Oola-Ong-Ua!"* The alien exclaimed as he pointed his left index finger at the floating debris and it began swirling around them quickly—so quickly a wind began roaring.

Alonzo came running up to FDR's wheelchair and grabbed. The soldier stationed outside entered as well, a Colt .45 pistol drawn. FDR sat grinning at the sight of the alien orchestrating the debris. "You boys stand down!" FDR snapped. "Let's see what Bandit is up to."

Vannevar turned to face Alonzo who was clearly concerned and he gave Alonzo a reassuring nod. Vannevar motioned for the soldier to stand down. But the soldier remained poised behind FDR and Alonzo. As the glass and debris swirled around Vannevar Bush and FDR as though they were in a wind tunnel, the alien then opened his right palm that had the melted, liquid hot metal inside of it from the coin and that silver metal oozed from his hand in a twisting line that reminded FDR of a snake moving in the grass. Soon, that metal found its way in the swirling debris cluster. Seconds later, the wind stopped and the debris formed into a clunky, rectangular shape with an outer layer of liquid silver from the quarter that flowed around the surface of the makeshift alien device like water.

The device hovered lazily before Vannevar Bush who stared in amazement. "The being does not only reverse engineer our disassembled technology," He marveled to himself.

FDR nodded. "It can build its own devices with our equipment." He concluded for Vannevar Bush.

"Most impressive!" Alonzo muttered while standing behind FDR. *"Scoot-Scoot-Mwa-Dunga!"* The alien commanded. Vannevar reached for the device and before he could grab it, the device floated over to

FDR and Bandit. Vannevar followed it. Bandit looked up at FDR. *"Ung tolo!"* He said, pointing. FDR smiled uncomfortably. "I can't understand you, Bandit." *"Ung tolo!"* Bandit repeated, pointing at the device he had constructed. FDR nodded.

"Mr. President, I would not—" Vannevar began but before he could finish, FDR had already grabbed the device.

Once FDR grabbed the device, blue electricity shot out and consumed the president.

"No!" Alonzo screamed angrily and moved forward to pull the president back. Before he could, however, an unseen force pushed Alonzo to the ground.

Vannevar immediately lunged for the device but the same unseen force that had pushed Alonzo to the ground now held Vannevar Bush in place. The soldier in the back was joined by three other soldiers who were immediately thrown out of the room and the steel door was slammed shut by an unseen force.

"Oooo..." Bandit muttered as these events occurred.

"I'm OK, boys." FDR murmured in an attempt to reassure his troubled staff. But his voice did not sound right. Rather than calm them down, FDR's voice and presentation just amplified the concerns of the staff more.

FDR did not care, though. He was in physical danger the longer he held onto the alien device. Yet, his mind was being transported to a place far away; a disjointed memory of an alien world. FDR was being given a warning of what was in store for the United States—for humanity—if they did not fully awaken to the realities of the space around Earth. And the images that the device flooded FDR's mind with were truly terrifying.

FDR awoke from what he assumed was a terrible nightmare. Some time must have passed from when he was in the bunker below the White House as he was now in totally different surroundings. The air was warm, like a mid-July day back in his palatial home in Hyde Park, New York. The sky was a dark blue, almost black, color. As FDR came to, he heard the familiar hoots and toots of Bandit. FDR's hands stung from where he was holding the device that Bandit had built in the bunker. But the device was gone. FDR looked around and realized he was standing in what looked like a desert. There was sand and rock everywhere—but it was unlike anything he'd seen before. The sand was coarser and darker and the rocks around him were an obsidian black. The air smelled strange, too; metallic. And it was quiet. Almost as though he were standing in a soundproof room or a radio booth.

FDR was jolted when that deep silence was penetrated by the sounds of high-pitched whining, as though some unknown machine had been activated in the distance, followed by the familiar sounds of massive explosions. In fact, whatever was transpiring in the distance was so forceful that the ground shook. Instinctively, FDR sprang up from the ground that he had been lying on, and was momentarily taken aback by the fact that he was standing. He looked down at his legs and marveled at the sight at seeing his once athletic legs supporting his body without any assistance from either metal braces around his legs or without the wheelchair that he had been bound to for so long. Ignoring the chaos occurring around him, FDR beamed at the thought of being able to stand, walk, and possibly run again.

The president's momentary excitement was broken by the repeated sounds of the high- pitched whining. Now that he stood, he saw over the obsidian cliff that he was standing on and saw in the valley below him the orange and yellow lights of a vast city in the strange valley below where he stood. The city was larger than any city he had seen. While he knew it was a city, FDR acknowledged that it was unlike any city he had ever witnessed. Its lights went on and on seemingly forever. It was sprawled out throughout the valley below much as Los Angeles was sprawled out, with twinkling city lights twinkling so far into the distance that they seemed to merge with the horizon beyond them. Yet, this city was far larger than Los Angeles—or New York, for that matter.

The buildings were unlike any building in either Los Angeles or New York. They looked like a combination of the glassy, obsidian rock that comprised the alien desert FDR was standing in but with sleek, silver metal interspersed within the obsidian rock along with yellowish lights. The city below was still, too. No one walking the streets or vehicles of any kind traversing roads. A robotic screeching could be heard echoing throughout the city that FDR immediately assumed was a form of alien alarm. When FDR looked up into the dark sky above the city, he realized that those alarms must have been the equivalent of air raid sirens. Directly above the city were strange crescent-shaped ships hovering silently directly over the buildings. They were an olive green, gold, brown, and gray color, with demonic red and orange energy firing from the underside of the craft—cutting down the buildings of the city in fiery explosions. FDR stared at one of the massive crescent-shaped spacecraft nearest to where he was standing and saw an emblem of a winged serpent emblazoned on the side of the crescent-shaped ship.

FDR was immediately reminded of the horrific images of London during Hitler's Blitz. He was unsure as to what was going on around him—and why—but he could tell that the city was under attack and he instinctively empathized with whoever lived in the city below just as he naturally stood with Churchill's Britain during its hour of need. Unlike London, though, there was no indication that the people who were under attack were mounting any kind of defense of their great city. It was simply being obliterated all around FDR. The city remained silent, save for the alien alarm that shrilled throughout the empty boulevards and roadways.

FDR quickly ducked as the tallest obsidian and metal building in the center of the city— what looked to FDR as a spire—was incinerated by a hellish red energy blast that seemed to simply melt the obsidian and metal that comprised the building. The destruction of that massive spire had devastating knock-on effects for the buildings around it. FDR thought that that strange building must have somehow linked the city together because as soon as it was destroyed much of the city began to implode. Dust and debris rose quickly from the valley that had once housed the alien metropolis. FDR began coughing and squinting as the dust from below rose to the top of the valley where he was standing, viewing the alien apocalypse. He reached in and pulled out a handkerchief adorned with the presidential seal on the bottom and covered his nose and mouth.

FDR turned to flee from the area, astonished that he had not woken up from whatever nightmare he assumed he was being subjected to. But when he turned around his heart almost stopped as he saw a nearly seven-foot-tall lizard-like creature standing before him. Its eyes glowed red and it bore its fangs out at FDR. The monster wore a golden mesh skin-tight uniform with a smaller version of the winged serpent proudly displayed on the reptile's right chest. The image reminded FDR of Hitler's Swastika. He knew that he was staring at one of the city's attackers. The creature hissed at FDR who stood totally captivated by its hellish appearance. He wished that the nightmare would be over. The strange beast raised his claws high in the air and started to lunge at FDR. When it did, it suddenly froze in place. FDR, who was waiting for the blows to rain down upon him from the beast in the hopes that he'd be awoken from his nightmare, was puzzled. He recoiled as he saw, standing behind the beast, a four foot-tall gray being that looked like a slightly taller and more mature version of Bandit.

The gray creature held out its arms. FDR knew that it was the reason for why the vicious man-like reptile did not complete its violent attack upon him. Then, another gray alien appeared from behind the one that was using its telekinesis to hold the reptile in place; it made a fist with its right hand and then twisted that fist in the direction of the reptilian beast. The reptile's body contorted awkwardly and the loud popping of all its bones could be heard being broken by the force of whatever power the gray aliens were using on the being. The reptilian then collapsed to the ground, dead.

The lead gray alien that had been holding the reptile in place reached his tiny left hand out for FDR to take. When FDR grabbed the hand, everything went silent. He could tell that the battle was still raging all around him. But he could hear nothing—save for his own breathing and the breathing of the gray alien that had embraced him.

"Wh-what is this?" FDR demanded.

The gray alien pulled FDR toward him and pointed at what looked like a floating brown crate. When FDR looked inside it, he recognized Bandit, sleeping within the protective confines of it. Immediately, FDR was overcome with a sense of hopefulness. This was not coming from within him, of course. It was being put on him by the powerful, four-foot-tall gray alien being who was holding his hand.

Instantly, the image of the burning alien city shifted and he was sitting alongside the gray alien and two of his compatriots inside a flying saucer. A three-dimensional image of Earth projected in front of them. FDR realized that he was not living through the present. He was seeing living history; a live record of how Bandit came to be on Earth. As FDR stared in awe at the image of Earth, he felt the seat that he was sitting in become tight around him. Suddenly, the walls of the circular control room they were in faded away and an image of a strange, alien hangar appeared.

What appeared to FDR to be a hangar door slowly opened in front of the saucer they were on. FDR glanced over at the gray alien who had held his hand. He saw that the aliens had placed their three tiny fingers into what looked like handprints on the seats next to them. When they did, the entire ship whirred to life. FDR looked beyond them to the side, where the steel-like wall had been replaced with a 360-degree panoramic view of the ship's surroundings. He saw a whole fleet of flying saucers readying to depart alongside theirs. He did not understand how he knew, as no words had been uttered since his arrival in this strange place, but FDR knew that they were leaving their homeworld and coming to Earth.

Two saucers, one to their left and one to their right, shot forward from the hangar only to be blasted into a million, tiny fiery parts. The gray alien who had taken FDR's hand and was clearly in command of this ship, looked back at the crate with Bandit inside of it. The alien nodded at it and then the saucer they were in shot forward.

The saucer quickly cleared the hangar and began ascending into the dark sky above. Red lights began flashing and FDR could see that several smaller crescent-shaped vehicles with the winged serpent logo on them were giving chase to their saucer. Electric green energy shot forth from the crescent-shaped vehicles that were pursuing their saucer. They had reached the upper atmosphere of the alien world and were now making wild zig-zagging movements, still climbing into the alien sky. Through the transparent wall, FDR could see what looked like were hundreds of other saucers rising from all around the alien world. FDR was mesmerized also by the fact that they were clearly now in space and that this world had three moons orbiting it.

FDR's focus was shifted away from the natural, alien beauty around him to the fact that the hundreds of other saucers fleeing from the stricken world were exploding as they got into space. FDR saw why: there was a fleet of continent-sized ships that looked like giant, scraggly space rocks—all with the winged serpent symbols on them—orbiting the alien world. They were picking off the fleeing saucers like it was a turkey shoot. FDR became enraged by this sight. He became especially irate as he realized that not one of the saucers was fighting back. Without thinking, he placed his hands inside the three-fingered handprints on the seat beside him, transforming his hand so that only three fingers were on where the three alien fingers should go. Not expecting anything to happen, FDR was surprised to see the console come to life momentarily. But when it did, the white light turned red, prompting the other two aliens to look back with concern at FDR.

From behind the saucer, the multiple smaller crescent-shaped ships that were madly firing their green energy weapons at the escaping saucer exploded suddenly. Several blasts landed on the underside of their saucer, causing the ship to shake and sparks to fly. The two gray aliens piloting the craft's eyes widened. FDR could tell they were extremely displeased with him. The other gray stood and charged over to where FDR was seated and reached down, pulling FDR's hands away from the handprint console beside his seat. The being was shaking his head and, while his face was expressionless, FDR could sense that the being was very upset at him. Just as a massive green energy bolt was coming from one of the larger alien ships in orbit, the gray alien who was piloting the vehicle, the one who had taken FDR's hand on the planet below, jumped the ship away from their dying world.

The next thing that FDR saw was the ship entering the Earth's upper atmosphere rapidly, out-of-control, clearly more damaged from the battle than their silent pilots had realized. FDR realized he was witnessing the events that led to the crash of the craft in Cape Girardeau. His eyes widened as he saw they were rapidly approaching a brown field. FDR knew the craft was coming to its end. He let out a wail of fear as he felt his heart stop. Just as the stricken vehicle was readying to plunge into the ground below, FDR believing everything was over for them, everything went black.

S*EVERAL DAYS LATER...*

FDR let out a scream. He immediately recognized where he was: the room where Alonzo and the White House physician routinely administered his doses of cocaine, which kept him going throughout the heaviest parts of his presidency thus far. FDR recovered his breath and leaned up as best he could, suddenly realizing that he was once again a prisoner in his own body. Somehow FDR knew everything that had happened to Bandit and his people; he understood what they were doing and why their city was being destroyed. They were being purged by the man-like reptilian creatures that he saw in the memory Bandit had exposed the president to.

"I know what happened to Bandit." FDR blurted out to no one in particular. "I know it all." He added solemnly.

"There, there, sir." Came the calm voice of Dr. George Draper, FDR's personal physician.

"Ah, doctor..." FDR began. "There was some concern about your health these last few days." Draper said ominously. FDR looked confused. "How long have I been asleep?" "Two days, almost." Came the curt voice of General Marshal. FDR's eyes widened. "That's not good, general." Marshal shook his head. "No, sir, it is not." He replied curtly. "Well, don't go swearing in my successor just yet!" FDR joked as Dr. Draper helped the president up. Alonzo moved in behind FDR and FDR looked relieved when he saw Alonzo. "How are you?"

Alonzo shrugged. "Oh, I'm fine, Mr. President!"

FDR looked Alonzo over, who seemed fine—albeit somewhat tired. "Were you...affected by whatever our little Bandit did?"

Alonzo shook his head. "I couldn't move neither could Dr. Bush for a few minutes but whatever Bandit did to us wore off fairly rapidly, sir."

FDR slapped Alonzo on the shoulder enthusiastically. "Thank, God!"

Marshal approached FDR with a stern look on his face. Unbeknownst to the president, Marshal and Draper were both trying to assess if FDR had been compromised by his contact with the alien in some manner. "You said you knew something about the creature, sir?" Marshal prompted.

FDR nodded happily. "Gentlemen, as badly as we've got it down here, it'd seem like it's much worse up there!"

Draper remained staring at FDR.

"Our little friend downstairs—Bandit—is one of the last of his kind." FDR said knowingly.

"Respectfully, sir, how can you know that?" Came the voice of Vannevar Bush, who had entered the room along with Harry Hopkins.

FDR smiled at his old friend. "Glad you could join us!" He said to Hopkins. Hopkins looked very concerned. "I could say the same to you, Mr. President." FDR chuckled. "I'm fine. Just fine." He said reassuringly. "How did you come by this intelligence, Mr. President?" Marshal asked firmly. "Bandit told me." FDR said nonchalantly.

Draper looked concerned and Marshal and Bush exchanged confused glances. "How, sir?" Bush asked from behind FDR.

"Well," FDR started and then looked annoyed. "Will you two come around where I can see you?" He demanded of Bush and Hopkins, who were standing at the door behind FDR. They instantly did as they were told. "That device that Bandit built from all that...junk you had assembled, Vannevar, that was how I saw it." FDR explained.

"Saw what, precisely, Mr. President?" Vannevar prompted.

"How Bandit's home was destroyed." FDR said distantly, remembering the traumatic events he had witnessed.

"You're saying the device is some kind of recording device?" Vannevar inquired, his mind racing trying to figure out how they could use that technology to their own advantage.

FDR looked lost. "No."

"How do you know Bandit's home was destroyed?" Draper asked, assessing FDR; trying to see if his president had been compromised psychologically by the alien.

FDR recoiled. "Don't look at me like that, George!" FDR snapped defensively. "I'm not crazy!" He insisted.

Dr. Draper smiled. "Of course not, Mr. President." FDR grimaced. "Well now you're just humoring me!" General Marshal stepped forward, boxing both Vannevar and Draper out. "Who are his people and who attacked them?" FDR stared at Marshal, remembering the winged serpent logo. "Big lizards." He said distantly. All the men exchanged confused looks. "Like something from a horror film." FDR said, shaking his head. "It looked like the

London Blitz—but with spaceships." FDR added.

"What did, sir?" Marshal inquired.

"Their great city was attacked by these lizard-men. Then these four-foot-tall gray beings—Bandit's parents, or caretakers, I think—took me to their flying disc." FDR said, realizing that he sounded insane. "There were hundreds of these ships and they put me onboard one with Bandit, who was in a crate of some kind, and we blasted away from their dying city—" FDR cut himself off as he realized his advisers were skeptical and likely getting ready to put their president in a rubber room. FDR softened for a moment. "Gentlemen, I am *not* crazy."

Draper nodded. "Mr. President, what you're saying is extraordinary."

"For the last few weeks we've had a being from another world living in the basement of the White House." FDR reminded them.

Hopkins stood quietly behind the rest of the group, taking in what the president was saying. He was concerned that the staff would think the president was insane. Hopkins did not want the alien and the president involved at all. But he feared that FDR's sanity may be questioned by some of the things he was saying.

"I saw the most incredible battle take place, not only on this strange alien planet, but in the skies and space above. And their ships. My God, the spaceships are…mortifying." FDR explained, gesticulating in a manner that made him seem manic.

Dr. Draper, who was a renowned physician who worked at the prestigious medical school at Columbia University was also a eugenicist who believed that science and medicine could determine someone's value to society. Hopkins noted that Draper was reviewing the president and Hopkins could tell that Draper was contemplating the idea that FDR had lost his mind. This could be a real scandal—and a significant complication for Hopkins' agenda.

Luckily, he'd taken steps to mitigate the threat that further contact with the alien posed FDR. While FDR was incapacitated, Hopkins authorized Vannevar Bush to transfer the alien far away from the White House; to the General Electric facility where the alien craft was being studied in Lynn, Massachusetts. Unbeknownst to either Vannevar Bush or George Marshal, the alien would never make it to the facility. Hopkins' Soviet handlers planned to intercept the package. This was not according to the plan that Hopkins had initially wanted, but FDR's interaction with the alien forced Hopkins' hand.

"And, gentlemen, I got the distinct impression that that was not merely a recording." FDR said, his comment hanging in the air.

"What does that mean, Mr. President?" Vannevar asked, sounding skeptical.

"I interacted with the people there. I even commanded one of their starships. I think I might have been the reason for why the aliens chose to come here…" FDR trailed and then rubbed his eyes. "Gentlemen, I…really should get some rest…" He trailed.

Dr. Draper smiled politely. "Of course, Mr. President." Draper then regarded Alonzo and motioned for him to assist the president into the nearby wheelchair. "Let's get you up to the residence." He added.

After FDR was placed into his wheelchair, Alonzo began wheeling him out. "Please do not think this is madness of some kind, men." FDR plead weakly.

"Just get some rest and get back to us, sir!" Draper called out.

As soon as FDR and Alonzo exited, Marshal glared over at Hopkins. "None of this goes into the public record." Hopkins said sternly to Draper, who was cleaning up the place.

"What?" Draper asked innocently. "What just transpired here." Marshal stated. Draper shrugged. "Nothing happened here as far as I'm concerned." He said nonchalantly.

Hopkins nodded, relieved that Draper was still aware of how important FDR was to their plans—and for the country. "Thank you, doctor." He muttered, relief coming from his voice.

"It's a good thing you authorized me take possession of the creature." Vannevar noted to Hopkins.

Hopkins nodded. Marshal shook his head. "It should be at my facility." Hopkins raised his hand reassuring. "It will be transferred once Dr. Bush and his team are done with it." Marshal scoffed. "C'mon, Mr. Hopkins, putting that thing anywhere near its craft is a bad idea!" Vannevar recoiled at that statement. "I couldn't disagree more, General. It might be able \to unlock the secrets of the downed craft faster than my team ever could!" "General, it sounds to me like Dr. Bush's team is at their wit's end with that spacecraft."

Hopkins noted. Vannevar concurred. "We can't make heads-or-tails of any of it." Marshal was annoyed. If that creature got near its ship, there was no telling what might happen. "Well, it's out of my hands for now." Marshal said in his short, clipped, military tone. "I assure you that my team will keep your people apprised of whatever we discover in our experiments." Vannevar said calmly. But Hopkins' mind was elsewhere. He kept checking his watch, knowing that the Soviet spies were readying to make their moves. He implored Mayor not to risk killing Americans; that would just bring the ire of the FBI down on them. Mayor had assured him that his team would be careful. At the same time, though, Mayor insisted that the FBI was not onto his spies. According to Mayor, the presence of the vast Nazi spy ring worked in their favor as the FBI was far more concerned about that. Still, Hopkins was not comfortable with this operation. He'd be happy when he knew it was over and he hoped above all that any injuries or deaths could be avoided.

Hopkins had given Mayor's team the train information that the alien was being transported on. Their plan was to ambush the train at one of the scheduled stops in Connecticut. Hopkins had no idea how the team planned on stealing the creature without getting into a firefight. He was gripped by worry.

"They just don't understand, Alonzo." FDR said sadly as he was positioned in his plush bed in

the upstairs residence in the White House. "If they could just see what I saw. Experience what I experienced." FDR continued.

"Yessir." Alonzo said. FDR looked up at his caretaker with skepticism. "What'd you experience?" Alonzo cocked his right eyebrow up. "You mean when I was under whatever spell that thing put me under?" FDR nodded.

"The world's biggest headache, sir." Alonzo said earnestly. "Like one whale of a hangover!" The White House butler joked, eliciting a hearty belly laugh from the president. "So you say that little guy is a refugee?" Alonzo asked, his thoughts drifting to the strange being that they had kept for weeks under the White House. FDR nodded. "I tell you, Alonzo, it sounds like the whole *universe* has gone made with war fever." He said, the caustic images of the alien city being decimated by the strange reptilian ships flooding into his mind. "They were trying to tell me something about Bandit." He said, clearly annoyed that he could not comprehend fully the message the aliens were trying to impart to him. "They were trying to warn me...or tell me..."

Alonzo finished tucking the tired president into his bed. "What's that, Mr. President?" FDR was frustrated. "I don't know, Alonzo." "You were with his parents, though, in the memory?" Alonzo prompted. FDR shrugged. "I really don't know what they were to him. I sensed that they cared for— even probably—loved him. He was..." FDR shook his head. "You said they came here because of you?" Alonzo asked, remembering what FDR had said when he had awoken downstairs. FDR grinned sheepishly. "I tell you, Alonzo, I don't think it was just a memory or some kind of living recording. I think I was actually there." He said, sounding confused. "How's that possible?" Alonzo asked skeptically. FDR thought about it for a long while. Perhaps these creatures could control time? The more FDR thought about that, the more frustrated he became. FDR threw his hands up in the air. "I really don't know, Alonzo."

Alonzo nodded sympathetically. "I'll tell you what: I don't think they were planning to stay here." FDR said. "Oh?" FDR nodded. "Their ship was damaged as it was fleeing. I think they came here to make repairs and then move on to somewhere else..."

"Do you know where?" Alonzo asked, genuinely interested in the prospect that there was more aliens out there.

FDR shook his head. "I got the sense that there was a big war going on and Bandit's people were just caught in the middle. Like Poland today." FDR elaborated, referring to the fact that Hitler's aim was never to simply take over Poland. It was to use Poland as a stepping stone into a much more strategically valuable region of Europe. FDR thought of the reptilian alien he saw. "Their attackers, though, make the Nazis look like wall flowers."

Alonzo's eyes widened. "That's pretty frightening, sir." FDR nodded. "And I tell you, I don't think we've seen the last of them. I really don't." Alonzo looked worried. "Oh, dear." FDR looked at Alonzo. "First thing when I'm feeling better is I go downstairs and find out more from our little friend." He said firmly. "Might I get a glass of warm milk with some nutmeg?" FDR asked.

Alonzo nodded. "Of course, Mr. President." Alonzo reached over to the nightstand and grabbed the phone to the White House kitchen and requested the president's order. He then stood up. "I'll be right back upstairs with it, sir."

FDR smiled. "Good man!" "Oh, and Mr. President?" Alonzo inquired. "Yes, Alonzo?" "Well, it's just...I don't think you'll be able to see your little friend anymore." Alonzo said ominously. FDR glowered in confusion.

"Mr. Hopkins had the being moved from the White House." Alonzo said, knowing that the was not supposed to reveal this information to FDR, as per Harry Hopkins' orders. But, Alonzo's loyalty was to his president. "He and General Marshal were very worried about your reaction to whatever the little guy put you through." Alonzo explained, trying not to totally throw the presidential advisers under the bus.

FDR was visibly upset. "Where'd they move him to?" He demanded. Alonzo wasn't sure he remembered so he shrugged. "To that facility up the road in Fort Hunt?" FDR prompted. Alonzo shook his head, racking his memory. "No, sir. Somewhere in Massachusetts." He said, although he was unsure of his answer. FDR knew exactly where they were transporting him. "Why on Earth would they put

Bandit with his ship?!" FDR demanded, feeling that once Bandit got near to his spaceship, he'd get inside of it, and leave.

"There was a polite argument between Mr. Hopkins and General Marshal about that very possibility, if I recall." Alonzo said. "But Dr. Bush interceded and agreed with Mr. Hopkins that the alien should go to their facility in Massachusetts." Alonzo explained, remembering more fully the events of the last 24 hours.

FDR let out a loud sigh. "Of course he did, Alonzo." He said in a disappointed tone. Alonzo put his head down. "I'll get that warm milk now, sir." FDR nodded. "Alonzo, the first thing I'm doing when I wake up is calling that damned facility to get my little Bandit back here!" FDR insisted. Alonzo was uncomfortable but said nothing. "I'll be back with the milk, Mr. President."

Alonzo said once more, exiting the room.

Fritz Joubert Duquesne drove the car over the train tracks in the Connecticut woods. It was dark, Duquesne's favorite time of the day to do his work. During the First World War, Duquesne had proven himself to be a master demolitionist. Throughout his time in South America, he favored bombs as his tool of espionage and assassination. Tonight was no different. He parked the car on the tracks and stepped out, flicking the cigarette he'd been smoking on the ground of the forest he was in. Duquesne then ran to the side of the tracks, where a group of his men—armed with knives, pistols, and automatic rifles—were hunkered down, waiting for the fireworks to begin.

Duquesne nestled into the grassy knoll that led up to the train tracks and as he did, one of his men, another German-American who posed as a dock worker, named Alfred Brokhof, handed Duquesne a Tommy Gun. Duquesne smirked and checked to make sure the weapon that had made American gangsters a decade earlier, like Al Capone, so infamous, was loaded. "Danke!" He whispered in gratitude to Alfred. "Our sources say that the target is in the fifth train car." Duquesne whispered. "We hit there first." He said.

The ground began rumbling and the blaring horn of an incoming train in the distance, getting nearer to where the men were hiding, could be heard. Duquesne nodded in excitement to himself. He pulled out a wired detonator from his pocket. "Be ready!" He commanded his team of spies.

The headlight from the train cut through the trees and darkness of the night as it rounded a corner, getting very near to where the men were. Their plan was to stop the train. To do that, Duquesne had blocked the railway junction with his car. Once the engineer driving the train saw the vehicle, the train would slow down. Not having enough time to stop entirely, the front of the train would crash into the parked car, which would only help to slow the vehicle down more. A secondary explosion on the tracks would then derail the train, harming or killing whatever American soldiers were inside the train, giving Duquesne's team of Nazis the time they needed to acquire the target and get it back to Germany.

Duquesne smirked to himself at the thought of the Soviet spy chief in the United States, Akhemov, realizing that his best laid plans had been circumvented by the Germans. The Soviets, Duquesne believed, were fools. They were no match for the power of the Reich and this escapade just proved it.

"Get ready, my friends!" Duquesne said to the group of his men. Most of them were not professional soldiers. He could sense they were scared. Combat, even covert warfare of the kind they were conducting behind-enemy-lines, was much different than stealing plans and information from the enemy as his spy ring had been doing for more than a year.

The train was within spitting distance of Duquesne and his men now. He knew the engineer driving the train saw the parked car. The horn on the train intensified in its blaring...to no avail. Duquesne's heart quickened as he knew the plan was working perfectly. The screeching of the train's air brakes resonated throughout the dark forest in rural Connecticut. There was nothing the train could do, though, to stop in time. A few moments later, the loud crash of metal on metal could be heard as the slowing train slammed into the parked car. Second after that, the car's fuel tank exploded, lighting the front of the train on fire. Screaming from the front of the train could be heard as the hopeless engineer dove from the train. He had caught on fire and landed in the grass nearby, rolling around and thrashing wildly.

The engineer's screams was too much for the team. One of the Germans, a man named Rolf, who was abnormally tall and looked like a farmer, stood and ran over to the burning engineer. He raised his pistol and shot the man dead. Duquesne was concerned that the soldiers inside the train would hear the gunshots so, without further delay, he detonated his perfectly laid bombs. The train tracks below the train erupted, sending the back portion of the train tumbling from the tracks.

It was chaos and destruction, just as Duquesne had envisioned it. His men instantly erupted in giddy applause. Duquesne, the ultimate swashbuckler, laughed proudly. After a few moments, the train settled in its place. The front and back of the train were burning. The back of the train was totally off the track, leaving the middle and front standing still on the tracks. Duquesne pulled out a pocket watch and saw the time. He knew that they could not linger. "Schnell!" Duquesne commanded in his native tongue. At that, the small team of German spies went charging to the train.

Two American soldiers had managed to exit the train car where it was suspected the target was being held. Duquesne took immediate aim with his Tommy Gun and squeezed the trigger, dispatching the Yanks. "Schnell! Schnell! Schnell!" Duquesne urged his men to the train, the thrill of battle rushing into his blood. He'd not felt this way in years.

The team reached the targeted train car and set up a perimeter while Duquesne placed a grenade in between the door and the handle. "Stand clear!" He ordered his men. Without another word, the door exploded open. Duquesne poked his fedora-wearing head inside the darkened car. Immediately, a shot from an M1 Grand Rifle rang out—just missing Duquesne's head, blowing his fedora clean off. Duquesne saw the American who had fired and realized the young man was delirious. Duquesne finished the desperate American off in no time. He waved his men inside the train. "We're looking for..." He trailed as he moved throughout the damaged train car and saw at the back a crate with a strange box inside the wooden crate. "That's it!" He yelled.

Paul covered him from behind. Rolf and another strong German spy entered the train car and lifted the damaged box and began taking it outside. A muffled moan could be heard from beneath one of the seats and a crumpled American soldier could be seen stirring. Paul raised his pistol and shot the American dead and began leading Duquesne off the train. Duquesne looked back at the dying American and shrugged saying, "Sorry, lads, but war is war!" With that, Duquesne jumped back outside and began marching with his men to their escape car which would take them to a nearby bay where they would deposit the crate onto a small vessel, which would then rendezvous with a U-Boat waiting just off the coast.

As the men ran into the forest where a car was waiting for them, Duquesne turned to face his loyal aid, Paul, and he said, "I'd love to see the look on Akhemov's face when he realizes we got to the train before he and his Soviet stooges could!"

Paul laughed madly at that thought. "Yes, Colonel, that'd be a sight to see!" He confirmed.

"Gentleman," Duquesne called after his team, "There's no way we can lose this war!" He said confidently, his men letting out a *Huzzah!* As they ran into the night, laughing proudly at their accomplishment.

FDR slammed his hand into his maple wood desk in the Oval Office after hearing from his advisers what had transpired in the woods of Connecticut the previous night. "I told you that Bandit needed to stay here!" FDR cautioned angrily, looking up at Hopkins in annoyance.

Hopkins lowered his head apologetically. "We were just trying to do right by you, Mr. President."

FDR nodded. He could not be mad at his team for very long. They all needed each other and they all had a mutual respect that transcended professionalism for each other. "I know, Harry." He said sympathetically. FDR then glared over at the FBI director who was standing in the corner of the Oval Office with his hands folded in front of him, looking unmoved. "Edgar, what do your people have to say about this?"

J. Edgar Hoover was a smooth operator. Having served as FBI director since the Coolidge presidency, Hoover was not someone any politician wanted to cross. Although, he and Hoover had a long and cordial history; an understanding, considering that FDR had been in DC far longer than any previous president in American history. "We have a line on the culprits, Mr. President." Hoover said cryptically yet confidently.

FDR's eyebrows went up at that. "Oh?"

Hoover nodded. "It is the assessment of my counterintelligence agents that this was the work of a Nazi spy ring that we've been tracking for months."

"You're actively tracking this spy ring?" FDR asked incredulously. If that were so, how did they have such free reign to be able to conduct a brazen attack on a US Army train as they did?

Hoover nodded in affirmation.

"And?" FDR prompted.

"We have a source inside of the spy ring who has been working with us. The problem is that the spy ring is using the German diaspora, as well as we believe to be the Japanese, to augment their capabilities and reach here in the United States." Hoover explained. "That's why we missed this attack, despite having a source inside the spy ring." Hoover added.

"Well what does your source say?" FDR asked. Hoover frowned. "About this attack? Gentlemen, you know the importance of the package!" FDR reminded them. Hoover looked frustrated. "Respectfully, Mr. President, I'm not aware of the contents of the package in question." FDR realized that he'd never read Hoover into the alien. "You're aware of the incident at

Cape Girardeau earlier this Spring?" Hoover nodded. "I'm aware that something crashed, and our government recovered that craft...but my people were systematically cut out from any further aspect of that investigation by the US Army intelligence corps." He said bitterly.

Marshal looked uncomfortable at the conversation.

"Well, Edgar, we had the lone survivor of that craft here." FDR said, trying to gauge Hoover's response.

"Where?" Hoover asked. "In the White House bunker." Marshal said. "It gave us—me—some pretty interesting information." FDR said. "And now, just when we got it doing what we needed him to do, the Nazis steal him away from us!" FDR said angrily.

Hoover shook his head. He hated when others kept secrets from him. Hoover always believed that it was he who was the true protector of the realm; only he had a legitimate reason and need to keep secrets. "Mr. President, this Nazi spy ring is the key to finding out the creature's whereabouts." Hoover said firmly.

Hopkins nodded and then stared at Hoover. "The greater question, Director Hoover, is how did this Nazi spy ring even find out about the creature?"

Hoover shrugged his shoulders. "Well, Mr. Hopkins, as I've been saying: this city is crawling with foreign spies and agents provocateurs."

Hopkins nodded.

"I suspect you might have a mole in your administration, Mr. President." Hoover said grimly.

FDR rolled his eyes. "Oh, Edgar, let's not go down this path again!" He said incredulously, remembering the last time Hoover tried to get FDR to go on a witch hunt against his own government.

Hoover shrugged. "Mr. President, how else would the Nazi spy ring have learned about this?"

FDR was silent.

"I find it difficult to believe that there's a Nazi spy high up in either this administration or the military." Hopkins chided Hoover.

Hoover shifted to look at Hopkins. "The Reds are everywhere. Why not the brown shirts?"

Hopkins shook his head indignantly. "We're not having this conversation again, Edgar." FDR decreed.

Hoover nodded. "Yes, sir, Mr. President."

Marshal glared angrily at Hoover. He loathed the idea of using state power to hunt down fellow Americans—government servants, no less—because of political differences. Marshal did not trust Hoover and understood that he was a creature of Washington, D.C., who had his own agenda. He did not trust Hoover and feared that Hoover was fashioning his FBI into a secret police of sorts.

"Luckily, Mr. President, my men are already onto this spy ring. If we take them down, we'll probably be able to figure out what they did with the creature." Hoover said confidently.

FDR nodded. "Good. Notify me constantly of your progress, please, Edgar." Hoover nodded. "Yes, Mr. President." Hopkins glared at Hoover. "If Hitler's people can get this creature to give them advanced technology..." "...It'd be the end of the American experiment!" FDR concluded darkly. Hopkins nodded in agreement. He set aside his guilt, knowing that it was his contact with the Soviet spies that must have tipped off their rival Nazi spy ring operating in Washington, D.C. Hopkins wished that he had taken better care to protect the truth.

"Mr. President," Hoover said with a devilish grin, "I always get my man!" FDR furrowed his brow and then said, "I just want my little Bandit back."

1944...

A giant, silver bell-like device with the black German cross painted on one side and a Nazi swastika painted on another rested in the center of a Stonehenge-like circle of concrete monoliths. Nestled deep inside the Polish forest, the Nazi proving ground known as Peenemunde was at the epicenter of Hitler's frantic effort to build his "Wunderwaffe" or, "wonder weapons." Everything from rudimentary atomic weapons technology to jet engines to the V2 Rocket were being tested at this site. Three men in black Nazi officer's uniforms stood at a safe distance away from the Stonehenge-like concrete slabs, wearing protective goggles.

SS-Obergruppenführer Hans Kammler stood in the middle of the three Nazi officers, with his black military cap cocked slightly to the right. He had semi-curly black hair and a long face and jowels. In his mid-forties, Kammler, unlike the other two men who stood beside him, was not a scientist (though he had studied engineering at university). Kammler was an administrator of extraordinary capabilities, or at least that was what his immediate boss, the head of the brutal SS, Heinrich Himmler, believed. He stood surveying the exotic vehicle with an air of detachment. To his right stood Werner von Braun, the genius behind the V2 Rocket program that was terrorizing the people of England, and to his left, stood a short, stout man in a brown suit with a red Nazi swastika pin on the lapel. This was the head of Hitler's atomic weapons program, the world renowned quantum physicist from Bavaria, Werner Karl Heisenberg.

In German over a loudspeaker, an officious officer announced, "Attention! Attention! Test flight in one minute!"

Dozens of armed soldiers milled about being followed by countless scientists in white lab coats. Heisenberg was visibly depressed, his hair standing high above his head, making him look to the disciplined Kammler as a madman. Meanwhile, von Braun stood poised, despite the fact that Kammler had been hounding the two men to complete this most important project for more than two years! Kammler got along with von Braun. He could not stand Heisenberg and had long suspected that the famed scientist was, in fact, working to sabotage the ailing Nazi atomic weapons program along with the rest of his science team. When Kammler had voiced his concerns to Himmler, he was quickly shut down by Berlin, who refused to believe that their favorite scientist was working against them.

"This had better work." Kammler threatened the two men. "I make no guarantees." Heisenberg quickly retorted. Kammler scowled. "It will fly." Von Braun said confidently.

Kammler shook his head. "That is not the problem with this device. The problem is *keeping* it flying."

Von Braun shrugged.

Kammler appeared cool and collected. Behind his eyes he was a sea of rage. Kammler was enraged by the indifference that the scientists showed for how poorly their beloved Fatherland was doing in this war. He was angry because he had long believed that their best-and- brightest were actively working against the interests of the Reich and, in recent months, working to preserve for themselves a place in whatever order they assumed would come after the Third Reich lost the war. So many of the purportedly brilliant men in Germany had come to the pathetic conclusion that they were losing the war. But, in Kammler's summation, Germany was not losing the war. They were losing the race for better weapons. If they could achieve Hitler's dream of building more advanced weapons, the war would enter into a new phase—a period in which the Nazis regained the upper hand and defeated the Allies.

"This is an entirely new domain of physics we are dealing with." Heisenberg said defensively.

"Every area of science is new to those who have never explored it before!" Kammler spat dismissively. "All that is required to master new science is the will." He said firmly, evoking his Nazi ideological indoctrination. "And I find your will to be most lacking in these matters." Kammler hissed angrily.

"The Fuhrer trusts me." Heisenberg said coolly. "Who do you think you are to challenge me in this way?" He goaded the Nazi.

"When you are speaking to me, here, I am speaking for the Fuhrer, Dr. Heisenberg." Kammler said in a threatening tone.

"Power up Die Glocke!" Von Braun commanded.

A low warble resonated from beneath the bell-shaped vehicle. Four chains tethered the vehicle to the ground since the Nazis had not yet figured out how to control the craft. A blue energy emanated from the bottom of the bell. It blasted off the ground, high above the Stonehenge concrete formation it had been sitting inside, the chains straining to keep the vehicle in place.

Kammler's jaw twitched as he watched the exhibit. He had seen this dozens of times before. The craft was sold to him as an anti-gravity vehicle that could bend space—and time— around its curved surfaces. Kammler was convinced that this vehicle could not only become the next-generation fighter craft that would down countless Allied bombers, possibly even forcing the Allies to discontinue their brutal air raids on Germany, but Kammler believed the vehicle might even be a time traveling device. At least that was what Von Braun had theorized. What was infuriating to Kammler was that the craft was not something that his team had developed. It was created by alien hands and it was based off of a damaged alien craft that the Nazis had uncovered in the Black Forest almost a decade earlier.

The Nazis had even captured a living occupant from the downed vehicle, but it was injured. They did their best to repair its wounds but all they managed to do was to slow down its death process. It was well enough that the Nazis under Kammler were able to convince the creature to help them, though like Heisenberg and some of the other Nazi scientists, Kammler suspected that the alien they had captured was passively resisting them. That was until the Abwehr presented his team with a gift from America: another alien. And as soon as the juvenile alien captured in America came around, the attitude of the older alien they had harbored since the Black Forest crash had changed markedly.

Initially, Kammler had desired for the aliens to get the alien craft they had captured repaired. It was determined that the aliens could not—or would not—do that. However, they did design and build Die Glocke. Yet, Kammler was beginning to think the whole thing was a distraction or a poison pill to lead he and his team down the wrong research path; eating up critical time and limited resources on something that'd never work all while the Americans and their allies moved in for the kill.

As he watched Die Glocke spin and bounce around the sky above the concrete structure, Kammler picked up the radio and screamed, "Increase the power!"

Heisenberg's eyes widened when he heard the Nazi issue that command. Von Braun shook his head. "No, Obergruppenführer! The capacitors are already at full power!" Von Braun shouted over the hellish screaming and otherworldly thudding the engines on the machine were making.

Kammler looked madly at Von Braun and pulled the radio handset away from the scientist. "Nothing great is achieved without risk, Doctor!" He yelled madly. Moving the radio handset to his mouth, Kammler commanded, "Increase capacitors to 200 percent!"

Seconds later, Die Glocke began moving erratically about the place. Kammler grinned, believing they may have gotten the device working as intended. In fact, after a brief moment of insane movement, Die Glocke slowed down and appeared to stabilize its flight pattern. Once it stabilized and hovered over the Stonehenge-like structure, its power levels off-the-charts, its hull glowed red and it started to disappear.

Its disappearing act piqued Heisenberg's interest, who pulled out a notepad and began taking feverish notes about what he was witnessing. Kammler stood stoically in front of the other two scientists, a sense of victory overwhelming him. Von Braun stared in shock as he cap blew off his head. He started laughing madly at the sight of the disappearing Die Glocke.

"Continue with power levels!" Kammler decreed, speaking into the radio handset. Just as he said that, though, massive sparks erupted from the power generators surrounding the complex. The lights flickered as the sound of an engine being powered down resonated throughout the massive complex. Immediately, Die Glocke began bouncing about erratically once more. It returned fully into view. Then, its blue engines went dark and the thing smashed loudly into the ground below. Heisenberg had ducked down and was covering his head with his arms while Von Braun had taken cover behind Kammler, who remained standing, his look of anger worsening. "Another failure." Kammler huffed bitterly.

Von Braun had finished collecting himself and shook his head spastically. "Oh, no, Obersgruppenführer! The amount of data we've collected from this incident will go a long way toward us understanding how best to use this weapon!" He insisted.

Kammler was unimpressed. He marched steadfastly toward the bell-like ship, which had steam rising from the rivets on the hull. Kammler wore black gloves, like many SS officers did. He quickly reached forward, grasped a scalding hot handle which felt hot even through his black leather gloves, and pulled up on the handle. Instantly, the hatch leading to the inside of the craft lifted open. As it lifted open, steam hissed out, followed by a flood of human blood and internal organs. The test subjects—Jewish slave laborers—had liquefied. Yet again, Die Glocke was not safe for human use.

Kammler lifted his boot as some of the liquefied remains got on them. He shook his head bitterly and turned to face Von Braun and Heisenberg, who was covering his mouth with a cloth from his pocket. "I want to see him."

Heisenberg and Von Braun both started to protest.

"That was *not* a request!" Kammler thundered. "The creatures are sabotaging us." He concluded angrily.

"But, Obersgruppenführer, why would these beings do such a thing?" Heisenberg asked, almost as though he were pleading for the lives of the aliens in their care.

Kammler's jaw was tightly sealed shut. "Sir, those two beings are our—" Von Braun began. "Our what, Doctor? They've given us nothing but grief!" Kammler shouted. "They constructed his entire craft for us, sir." Von Braun said. "You mean they've misled us!" Kammler snapped.

Heisenberg was disgusted by the Nazi officer and did not mask his opinion. "You are a fool, Obersgruppenführer, to think that you could even threaten these beings."

Kammler's eyes widened and he moved closer to Heisenberg, gripping the handle of his Lugar pistol which was housed in its holster on his belt. "Who are *you* to speak to me in such a way? Unlike you, doctor, I've not surrendered in this war!"

Heisenberg scowled. "For the record, I strictly oppose your decision to harass and threaten these beings in our care."

"And you, Dr. Braun?" Kammler prompted.

Von Braun lowered his head as he felt Heisenberg's glare fall upon him. Von Braun looked up at Kammler and nodded. "I concur with your judgment, Obersgruppenführer. These beings may prove to be a security threat that we must assess."

Kammler smiled while Heisenberg chortled.

"Although, I'd also like to go on record voicing my concern that you may inadvertently harm or kill these creatures and that will set our efforts back significantly." Von Braun added.

Kammler was incensed by Von Braun's hedging. "You are dismissed." Kammler whispered madly to the two scientists. He then motioned for two SS guards to approach him. "Come with me." He hissed.

The door to the concrete cell that housed the two aliens at Peenemunde squealed open, revealing an irate Obersgruppenführer Kammler flanked by two armed SS soldiers. Kammler stared at the two, tiny gray aliens sitting on the floor inside. The older gray alien, who had been their captive since 1938, had black pock marks across his skin and his skin was dry and wrinkled whereas the other alien, the one they captured from America, appeared otherwise healthy. The German scientists had nicknamed the two "Hansel" and "Greta", though it was rumored that the younger alien that they called "Greta" was called "Bandit" by FDR.

Kammler gripped his pistol and pulled it out menacingly. The two aliens stared emotionlessly at him and then he plopped the gun into an unseen box on the outside of the room. He motioned for his guards to leave their weapons there as well. The Nazis had learned the hard way what happens if they brought weapons near the aliens—the older one, Hansel, used his mind to turn those weapons against the Nazis. Kammler would use his fists anyway, if necessary. He entered the room.

"The test failed." Kammler said bitterly to the alien they called Hansel. The two aliens stared at Kammler silently. *You failed us! Again!* Kammler screamed, clenching his right fist. The aliens remained staring at him, the older one barely able to stand after the torture it had been subjected for years under Nazi care. *"You!"* Kammler hissed marching toward the older alien. *"You did this!"* He screamed.

As Kammler approached the dying adult alien nicknamed Hansel, preparing to beat him, the smaller one that the Americans called "Bandit" and that the Germans called "Greta" began throwing its hands in the air, making an assortment of strange hooting and wooping noises, as if to get Kammler's attention. Kammler had been intrigued that the younger, healthier one tended to make so many vocalizations whereas Hansel never once uttered a sound. Hansel, despite being featureless, had what Kammler thought was the same empty, defeated look that so many of the victims of Nazism had at their hand. This gave Kammler a bit of perverse pleasure, knowing that he could inspire such fear on the pathetic races both on Earth and, obviously, from beyond. All he had to do was to provide his leadership with the weapons to keep the war going and he firmly believed that the Nazis could prevail.

Once Bandit tried to intercede, Hansel became animated in ways not seen since when the creature was first captured in the Black Forest. He began shaking his head back-and-forth, screaming *"Un-Lat-O!"* at the younger one. The guards moved in and grabbed Bandit roughly, prompting Hansel to let out a hiss. The lights began to dim as though another test of Die Glocke were occurring and the whole room began to shake violently. Hansel's eyes glowed white and a blue energy began forming in the center of Hansel's chest. The creature's ragged fists were clenched tightly and he stared intently at the two SS guards who were manhandling Bandit. The energy that had gathered around Hansel's chest shot out like lightning and hit the two SS guards, the explosion from the impact also knocked Kammler off his feet. Kammler, remembering that he did not have pistol on him, reached into his right boot and pulled out a Nazi dagger. He was going to kill Hansel.

The two SS soldiers were dead and on the floor. Bandit was freed from their oppressive grip. Hansel had also crumpled to the floor, weakened from using his limited energy the way he did to protect the child who, unbeknownst to the humans, was their species' only hope for survival. He was but one of only a few children who survived the purge of their homeworld by the reptilians. Like the rest of his species, Hansel understood that he had to protect Bandit with his life. That urge to protect the child was why Hansel gave into the Nazi demands and constructed a craft for them. Yet, as Kammler was starting to realize, Hansel had tricked the Nazis. Instead of simply repairing his ship that had crashed—something he could have done with the tools the Nazis had made available to him—Hansel destroyed his ship and built for the Nazis a device that would surely kill any human that tried to pilot it, depriving these awful humans of any chance of dominating either this world or the stars. The last thing the universe needed was another band of murderous beings ravaging the stars, as the reptilians currently were.

Kammler went to stab the downed Hansel when suddenly the steel in his knife simply liquefied and, like water flowing from faucet, dripped over toward the waiting hands of Bandit, which were extended out and maneuvering in a way that indicated to Kammler that the small being was manipulating matter. Next, Bandit took the liquid steel and fashioned them into what looked like bullets and arrayed them in what Kammler assumed was an attack formation. Instantly, Kammler's façade of being the dominant, tough guy dropped away and he screamed, *"Please, my friend, I'm just following orders!"* And began groveling and wimpering before the empowered juvenile alien.

Before Bandit could complete his innovative attack against the evil Nazi, though, Hansel lifted his weary head from the concrete floor and raised his left hand, waving it once. As soon as he did that, the steel turned to liquid again and splattered on the floor before Bandit. Bandit turned to face Hansel with a confused look. What the humans did not know was that this species of tiny gray aliens were pacifists. They were forbidden from using violence as part of their cultural code. Even in self-defense, these beings had strict rules to follow and since his cellmate was a juvenile who had not been properly acclimated to their ways—and with their homeworld having been destroyed—the juvenile was dangerous to anyone around him, including himself.

Hansel took this moment to teach the young one an invaluable lesson: any violence he employs would become like an addictive substance. Once the young began using his powers to hurt, no matter how noble his reasons may have been, the juvenile would seek to dominate others with that power.

Hansel stood up, slowly, knowing his time was limited before his body completely shut down. He limped over to the two downed SS guards and closed his eyes, motioning his tiny hands over their bodies. Seconds later, the two men awoke, perfectly healed, save for the scorch marks on their uniforms. The only reason Hansel had used his power on the two humans was because, with so few of his species having survived the purge, all juveniles had to be protected at all costs. This was one of the times their pacifistic code had to be abrogated—and immediately restored thereafter.

Kammler stood slowly and watched as the two shocked SS guards stood as well. He looked at them and shook his head in disgust. Kammler then smirked madly as he recognized the true power that these tiny beings wielded. Now, more than ever, he wanted to harness that power and claim it for the Reich. He knelt beside Hansel, who was sitting, weakly on the floor and pointed at him. "Now, you have my attention, Hansel." He then looked over at Bandit, or Greta as the Germans called the juvenile, and laughed sadistically. "And now I know what compels you. A child." Kammler was completely self-satisfied at this point. "You will give me what I seek. Because if you don't, my friend, one way or another, the child will suffer."

The tiny gray alien nodded. They did not understand the human language anymore than the humans understood theirs. These grays, like their taller cousins from Zeta Reticuli who were the primary targets of the reptilian's war, were empaths; they could understand what another being was saying or thinking by their emotions. And having spent almost a decade with these humans, Hansel had picked up some of their nonverbal mannerisms.

"When I return here, you will make Die Glocke work properly." Kammler demanded of the alien.

Hansel nodded.

Kammler stood and pivoted, marching quickly toward the door. The guards continued to compose themselves. The clanging sound of Kammler retrieving his pistol could be heard. He placed his black luggar in its belt holster as the two delirious guards slowly retrieved their machine guns and slung them around their shoulders.

Bandit had moved alongside Hansel, who was weak and dying and placed his hand over Hansel, who immediately slapped it away. Bandit was far too young to try to save the old and dying tiny Hansel. The attempt would kill them both. Only adults could try such a risky procedure. As the two aliens watched the humans collect themselves just outside the door, Kammler glared at the two aliens. He slyly reached down, pulled his pistol out, and shot the first guard in the heart and then the second one in the face. They fell outside the door. Kammler smiled viciously at the two aliens and then slammed the steel door shut.

Kammler exited the fortified bunker where the aliens were housed and saw Lieutenant Alois

Handel standing, waiting for him. The lieutenant snapped a sieg heil salute, which Kammler dutifully returned. Handel then gave a piece of paper to Kammler, who unfolded it and read it. The communications office had received a call from Kammler's nominal boss in Berlin, Heidrich Himmler, urgently requesting to speak with him.

The two men marched to the communications office and Kammler entered a smaller office for classified calls. He picked up a black handset and instructed the operator to patch him through to Himmler. After a few brief moments, Kammler heard the distinct breathing of Himmler on the other end.

"Heil Hitler!" The SS director, Himmler, hissed into the phone.

"Heil Hitler!" Kammler returned. "To what do I owe this honor, Reichsführer?" Kammler asked, a tinge of nervousness coming over him.

"Ja, what is this I hear about you interrogating the visitors?" Himmler barked.

Kammler's brow furrowed as he tried to determine just who leaked what was transpiring to his boss in Berlin. Before another word could be said, Kammler rolled his eyes as he realized it was Heisenberg.

"Hello, Kammler?!" Himmler impatientluy demanded.

Kammler puckered his lips in anger and then calmed himself, gripping the handset in anger so tightly that his knuckles turned white. "Yes, Reichsführer, I am here!" He replied.

"And?" Himmler prompted. Kammler sighed. "We had another setback with *Die Glocke,* sir." *"Ja, this is what I have been told."* Himmler said nonchalantly. *"The test subjects were still liquefied, eh?"* Himmler inquired darkly. Kammler nodded. "They were, sir." Himmler could be heard letting out a low chuckle. *"A little lesson from my farming days,*

Obersgruppenführer: always have a pair of spare boots at the ready!"

Kammler smirked. "Of course, sir."

"Now, you are to leave our visitors alone!" Himmler commanded. *"Their value is immense. Especially now that the Allies have landed in France."* He insisted.

Kammler winced at the thought of the Allies making their way onto sacred German soil. "Respectfully, Reichsführer, that is all the more reason for me to find out why the device is not functioning."

Himmler was silent. *"Killing our visitors serves no purpose for us."*

Kammler had to tread lightly here. He did not want his superior, the second-most powerful man in the Reich, to think he was being insubordinate. "Of course, sir. I was—"

"You were merely trying to serve myself and the Führer. I understand that. But you are risking everything with these antics. And you are upsetting Heisenberg and the other scientists in whom the Führer has placed great faith." Himmler said.

The mention of Heisenberg's name made Kammler's skin crawl. He would make the shifty scientist pay for having pulled an end-run on him.

"We are growing very concerned about your apparent lack of progress, Kammler." Himmler said matter-of-factly. *"If you are unable to execute your assignment, while regrettable, we will have you reassigned."* Himmler threatened.

Kammler stiffened. "That won't be necessary, sir." He reassured his boss.

"Fine. Fine." Himmler responded. *"Redouble your efforts. But do not harm the visitors!"* Himnler ordered and then slammed the phone down.

Kammler processed what he was ordered and then returned the black handset to the receiver and opened the door to the private booth. He saw Heisenberg and Von Braun standing in the tiny communications hut, with pale looks. Kammler scowled.

"You're stuck with me." Kammler blurted.

"Which one did you kill?" Heisenberg asked in a somber tone.

"Neither of them." Kammler replied. "But the Reichsführer informs me that *you* are trying to kill my career!" He accused.

Heisenberg looked confused. "By calling him and accusing me of overstepping with the visitors." Kammler explained. Heisenberg shook his head. "I never called the Reichsführer." He said innocently. Kammler did not believe Heisenberg and rolled his eyes. He then regarded the quiet Von

Braun suspiciously. "Not me!" Von Braun insisted. Kammler scowled. "I do have one standing order from the Reichsführer…" He trailed. "And?" Heisenberg prompted. "In light of your recent failures to get *Die Glocke* functioning and safe for human use, I am to redouble our efforts." Kammler said. "What will you two need for that?" "More power." Heisenberg said grimly. "More test subjects." Von Braun said sadly. Kammler smiled. "More Jews, you mean. Fortunately for us, we've got them in abundance. You will have as many as you need to experiment on." After that remark hung in the air between them, Kammler snapped a sieg heil salute. The two men returned the gesture after a brief pause.

Special Agent Patrick Greaves was excited because the intercepts coming from Nazi Germany into the United States indicated that something big was going on related to their experimental weapons program. After helping to arrest the Duquesne Nazi spy ring, the FBI counterintelligence center had managed to set up a fake Nazi spy ring that communicated with Nazi intelligence in Germany over shortwave radio. Thinking that Greaves and his fellow FBI agents camped out in a house in upstate New York were actual Nazi spies in the United States, the Abwehr shared many bits of information that were a goldmine for the Americans. The FBI was prevented from deploying in the wartorn regions of the world, so it fought the war at home against espionage agents and it also worked to stop the Axis Powers from undermining the United States in Latin America.

Greaves had split his time between the mission in upstate New York and Brazil, where so many Nazis were operating. Yet, the caustic events of Cape Girardeau in 1941 were never far from his mind—especially because his boss, J. Edgar Hoover, had put him in charge of the FBI's search for the lone survivor of Cape Girardeau crash that everyone assumed was kidnapped by the Nazis. For three years, Greaves had investigated the matter and had nothing but false leads. Finally, today, information was coming in about visitors at the Nazi missile proving ground in Peenemunde, Poland.

Greaves consulted with his team in the farmhouse and then decided to call Washington, D.C. Once he informed Director Hoover what he and his team thought they had stumbled across, all Hell broke loose in Washington. Greaves was on a train two hours later bound for the White House, wearing his Sunday's best. This kind of movement was pretty normal for Greaves. He'd spent the last year chasing Nazi spies in South America. Even before he joined the Bureau, he went to West Point and was a lieutenant in the Army. The only reason he had gotten out of the Army was because he joined it in peacetime and grew bored. Sensing that the real action was on the homefront, he applied and was quickly inducted into the FBI, where he rose rapidly in its ranks to become a senior agent with the Counterintelligence Center.

Greaves was smart but he was also a player. He rose fast because he was highly adept at knowing when to keep his mouth shut—and who he needed to throw under the bus to get there. A man in his late thirties, he was starting to be viewed with some degree of suspicion because he had not yet married. With the war on, though, Greaves was able to skirt that issue. He assumed that he was one promotion away from being stable enough to be able to finally settle down. But Greaves wanted to be strategic; he did not want to marry just any dame. He wanted to marry one with the right connections and family name. Greaves had ambitions that transcended the FBI.

And now here he was, standing outside the Oval Office, waiting to be called inside where he would brief the president. He smirked confidently to himself at the mere thought of his meteoric rise in the government. From field agent to this, all in a matter of ten years. Maybe in another ten years he'd be a permanent fixture here? Greaves had to play his cards deftly but he was certain he could.

The door to the Oval Office opened and the president's secretary stepped out. She eyed Greaves and smiled. He returned the smile. "They're ready for you now, Agent Greaves."

Greaves was frozen in place. He grabbed the knot at the top of tie and squeezed. "How do I look, dear?" He asked.

Missy winked at him. "You look great." She said reassuringly.

Greaves raised his eyebrows quickly and had his confidence restored. "Thanks, doll." He said and entered the Oval Office. When he had entered the Oval Office, he found Harry Hopkins sitting beside the president at his desk in a rumpled suit, looking as though he'd not slept for some time. FDR sat at the center of the desk in his wheelchair, he too, looked haggard and he puffed on cigarette that was dangling from a black cigarette holder, which hung lazily out of his mouth. Generals Marshal and William "Wild Bill" Donovan of the Office of Strategic Services (OSS), America's foreign intelligence service whose very existence rankled Greaves' grumpy boss, J. Edgar Hoover; Greaves saw the secretaries of war and state seated at the couches as well. Standing in the corner, watching the whole meeting unfold was a grim looking Hoover who was clenched onto a binder with the FBI logo on it and had a frown on his face.

"And, uh, who, pray tell, is this?" FDR called out as he saw Greaves gingerly enter the room.

Hoover glanced over at saw Greaves. "This is Special Agent Patrick Greaves of my Counterintelligence Center, the CIC."

FDR smiled. "Some bang up work your boys have been doing against those Nazis in South America!" He said proudly.

Greaves shrugged, feigning modesty. "Your very kind, Mr. President." FDR furrowed his brow. "I'm not being kind, Agent Greaves. Just stating the facts." Greaves nodded. "Yes, sir." Hoover glowered briefly at Greaves and then looked back at FDR. "I do recognize your name, Agent Greaves." FDR said. "Sir?" Greaves asked nervously. FDR nodded in affirmation. "Yes, from a very intriguing report from the Spring of

'41..." He trailed. Greaves immediately remembered and focused on FDR like a bird of prey focused on its next meal. No one was supposed to talk about that incident. While FDR was the president, Greaves had assumed that the Cape Girardeau affair would have been kept quiet even to the president, given Hoover's penchant for total secrecy as a form of exercising his complete control over sensitive national security matters.

"Agent Greaves believes he's got a significant lead on our friend." Hoover said cryptically, appearing uncomfortable with the discussion.

FDR nodded slowly. "Have you found my Bandit?" Greaves was puzzled by that comment. "The survivor." Marshall grunted under his breath. Greaves then nodded. "I think we have, sir."

FDR smiled. "Is he alive?" He asked, lowering voice and speaking in a tone of deep concern.

Greaves glanced at Hoover, prompting FDR to look annoyed. "Agent Greaves, you're talking to me not to Director Hoover!" FDR thundered. "It sounded on the intercepts like the Nazis have him and that he is, yes, alive." Greaves said trying to figure out whether he was upsetting his boss, Hoover, who would make Greaves pay if Greaves did anything that affronted Hoover.

"Where is he?" Hopkins asked from beside the president.

"We assess that he's being held at one of the Nazi missile proving grounds. A facility that's located in Poland's hinterland known as Peenemunde." Hoover said, cutting off his subordinate. "Wild Bill" Donovan was a bull of a man. He was tall with wide shoulders. The epitome of an American warrior. He stood and began distributing a one page document to the men assembled in the Oval Office. Hoover gritted his teeth and shot what Greaves interpreted to be a death glare as Donovan quickly handed the materials out. Greaves received one as well and he could see that it was a breakdown of what Peenemunde was.

"This is where they're launching the V2s that are plaguing Winston from!" FDR gasped, perusing the document.

"That's correct, Mr. President." Wild Bill said authoritatively. "We also think the facility has a role in Hitler's atomic weapons program." He added, knowing that this would pique the president's curiosity. Donovan bit his lower lip and then added, "And our pilots have been reporting strange objects flying from the direction of the facility during bomber raids." Donovan added uncomfortably.

FDR grinned madly, puffing on his cigarette. "Yes! The foo fighters!" He said, eyes widening playfully. "We're taking these reports seriously now?"

Marshall leaned in and said, "We have to, sir. There's simply too many reports coming in from both our people and the Brits."

"It's little Bandit. It has to be!" FDR insisted. Hopkins looked confused. "So he's helping the Nazis develop advanced weapons?" FDR frowned. "Have these foo fighters damaged our birds at all?" "Reports indicate that some have interfered with the electrical equipment on some of our bombers, but no, sir." Donovan said. FDR shook his head. "Bandit has been kept there for years now. He's probably being forced to build things and do God knows what!" FDR said sadly. "Those monsters have probably tortured him." FDR said angrily. "After everything that little guy has been through too…" FDR quipped, remembering the caustic images he had viewed after Bandit had built the device.

Greaves looked befuddled but nodded slowly.

FDR composed himself, took another puff of his cigarette, and then smiled at Greaves. "When do you head out to Europe?" He asked Greaves.

Greaves' eyes widened. "Uh…" Donovan looked offended. "Sir, FBI isn't operating in the war zone—" Hoover glanced over at the imposing Donovan. "No thanks to you and your OSS misfits." FDR put his hands up, as if to calm situation. "All right, gentlemen, we don't have time to fight a war in here as we're fighting the war out there." Hoover and Donovan nodded and said nothing. "Greaves. Do you have any military experience?" FDR inquired. Greaves nodded. "I served in the Army, sir. Before the war." "Agent Greaves was previously a lieutenant who graduated from West Point." Marshall muttered. Greaves smiled at Marshall and nodded. "Yes, sir. And I received training at the Infantry

School at Fort Benning when you were the assistant commandant there, sir." Marshall returned the smile. "I know, son." "Okay. So not a total naif." FDR ruminated. The room was silent while FDR contemplated how next to proceed. "Mr. President, I can assemble a team and try to get into Peenemunde within the week."

Donovan interjected. FDR nodded. "That's exactly what I want you to do, Bill." Donovan nodded, believing the meeting was over. "Yes, sir." "With Agent Greaves here—or, should I say Lieutenant Greaves—on the team." FDR said. Donovan recoiled and Hoover smiled briefly, sensing a victory. "Congratulations, Lieutenant Greaves, you are now an agent of the OSS! Good luck and

God bless! And bring my Bandit back." FDR ordered. "Every moment he's in the Nazi's custody, he's a threat to our war effort." FDR added solemnly.

"Very good, Mr. President." Greaves said, feeling uncomfortable. This is not what he wanted. He was quite pleased to remain stateside and work on his career.

Donovan approached with a sullen look on his face and tapped Greaves on the shoulder. "Welcome to the OSS."

Greaves shook Donovan's hand. "Thank you, sir."

Hoover approached the two men from behind. Donovan looked at Hoover and said, "Well, Greaves, you're mine now. Report to me tomorrow morning at 0730!"

Greaves nodded. "Yes, sir!" His prior military training flooding back to him. "Edgar." Donovan muttered as he exited. Hoover said nothing. Greaves and Hoover exited the Oval Office together. "Well, Director Hoover, it was a pleasure to serve—" Hoover recoiled. "Oh, I'm not done with you yet." Greaves' eyebrow lifted in confusion. Hoover grabbed Greaves' left shoulder and gave him a faux reassuring squeeze. "You're still one of mine, Patrick."

"Sir?" Greaves was confused.

"You think you're the only Bureau agent to go work for Donovan? I've got my people all over the OSS." Hoover said in a whispering, conspiratorial voice. "And now you're going to be my golden boy." He said maniacally. "This mission they're sending you on…it's the only one that counts. I want intel on everything the Nazis are up to at Peenemunde." Hoover said firmly. "I want regular reports to me." Hoover hissed.

Greaves nodded slowly.

Hoover shook his head. "Roosevelt," Hoover said bitterly. "None of these politicians get it." He said angrily. "The communists are everywhere." He whispered. "They've infiltrated every layer of Roosevelt's government. The OSS is full of the Red menace." Hoover said, sounding like a madman to Greaves. "But then you know that. You've been working counterintel for me since the start of this."

Greaves did know that there was much penetration of their government by foreign spies. But he had difficulty believing that the premier American spy agency, the OSS, had been that thoroughly compromised. "How will I get reports to you?"

Hoover grimaced. "You're one of the best counterintelligence agents in the country. You'll figure it out." He said dismissively. Hoover then angrily shoved his right index finger in Greaves' chest. "We cannot let the OSS get a hold of that technology or the visitor. They'd just be handed over to Stalin!" Hoover explained. "Well, not on my watch!" He added, gritting his teeth in determination. "I've been fighting the Reds my entire career. And after this war is over, they'll be next." Hoover said firmly. "And you're going to be my eyes and ears out there." Hoover added. "You got that?"

Greaves sensed an opportunity to play some of the most powerful people in America during one of the most severe crises in its history to his advantage. He nodded. "Of course, Director."

Hoover smiled like a predator once more and slapped Greaves' back. "Good hunting."

United States Army Air Corps Captain Hank "Spinner" Clark of Charlottesville, Virginia looked out at the night sky over Germany below his A-20 Havoc bomber. Assigned to the legendary 415th Night Fighter Squadron operating out of Southern France to support the Allied invasion of Europe from Normandy, Clark was tasked with a very special mission this evening. Clark piloted the A-20 that was escorting a team of six OSS commandos into Germany where they would assault a Nazi secret weapons production facility.

"All right, men, pucker up!" Clark shouted into his headset, knowing that by now the Nazi air defenses were alerted to their presence. All they needed to do was to escort a lone transport plane through the heavily fortified area of German territory nicknamed, "Naziland", where the elite OSS team would parachute under the cover of darkness to the secret Nazi proving ground in Peenemunde.

Once Clark gave that warning to his flight of ten A-20 Havoc bombers belonging to the legendary Army Air Corps 415th Night Fighting Squadron, who was escorting the transport plane, the flak started exploding all around their planes. "Let's get this show on the road!" Clark commanded. "Stay on target!" He urged his planes as the chatter of the pilots and their crews increased over the radio. Clark smiled, he loved this.

"Okay," Clark said into his headset, speaking with the pilot of the lead transport, "We're in Naziland! We're going to distract the Krauts as long as possible while you follow the pre- arranged flight path! You should be through this muck in a few minutes!" Clark shouted.

The A-20 Havocs veered to their right, taking much of the attention of the Nazi air defenses with them, giving the lone transport plane a chance to get through unscathed. The A20s soon began dropping their payloads on the ground below, lighting up the ground and turning it into a fiery hellscape. The pilots cheered across the radio frequency as their bombs were scoring major hits on the air defenses and infrastructure below.

Patrick Greaves marveled at how quickly his life had changed. He went from being a rising star at the FBI's Counterintelligence Center to now being coopted into America's foreign intelligence and espionage service, the OSS, and found himself flying behind enemy lines in Europe. His jaw twitched nervously and he did his best to hide the fear that was consuming him. If he could survive this ordeal, Greaves was convinced that the world would open to him professionally. As he looked around at the small team assembled around him, though, his fear grew. Most of these men, despite having military ranks, were *not* soldiers—and it'd been years since Greaves was under arms. Plus, as a newcomer to the OSS, Greaves was viewed with a degree of suspicion that he was unused to.

Sitting beside Greaves was the OSS commander of the mission, US Army Captain James Marks, a legendary OSS operative, who was rumored to have successfully ventured behind enemy lines a total of seven times and rescued Jewish scientists who could be helpful for the American war effort. He was also a skilled assassin, having killed multiple senior SS officers in the last year alone. Marks had made the jump into Normandy along with the 82nd Airborne and was one of the few men who had helped those American troops, who had been blown off course in the chaos of the nighttime drop, get to where they needed to be for when the main thrust of the Allied invasion of Normandy had begun.

Marks was a graduate of Yale University and had famously been the university's quarterback during his time at the school. Marks had spent two years living in Germany before the war. In fact, Marks had a German wife, meaning he was fluent in the language and a master of blending in. Despite his experience, Marks still looked like the young 19-year-old football quarterback he'd been 15 years earlier. He carried himself with an air of confidence that bordered on the absurd; breezily moving through combat while giving one a breakdown of Nietzsche's *Thus Spoke Zarathustra*.

The transport shook as flak shells exploded on the right side of the plane. Luckily, it was still far away—much farther away than what the pilots of the A20s were experiencing as they dropped their bombs on the heavily defended Nazi positions below. From the front of the McDonald-Douglas transport plane, in the cockpit, the men could hear the intense chatter between the pilots of the A20s; the battle was rough, and they had already lost two planes. Although, as Greaves glanced out the window, he could tell that their transport was moving away from the hectic battle rapidly. The Nazis did not see them.

On the other side of Greaves was a thin, 20-year-old Japanese-American, Corporal Takeuchi Itijima. The team referred to him as "Taki." At his feet was a large, black radio system that he would wear on his back like a backpack once they made it to the forest where the Peenemunde proving ground was located. He was reading from a small, pocket-sized Bible that was written in Japanese. A native of San Francisco, Takeuchi had been arrested and sent to an internment center in the desert. However, Taki was no Japanese spy. He was a Christian, like his parents, and he volunteered to enter the military as soon as he was of age. He spoke five different languages—including German and Polish—and was a technical wizard. He was an upstanding member of the OSS and would serve as the communications officer on this mission.

Across from Greaves was Sergeant Major Donny "Fireball" O'Shaughnessy of New York. An Irishmen by birth, O'Shaughnessy was an explosives expert. His hair was a fiery red and he had a red mustache. Standing at 5'11, he could bench press three times his weight and was a reputed drinker. His father had been an anti-British firebrand back in Ireland and, when they emigrated to the United States, his father was a low-level enforcer for the Irish mob that got involved with bootlegging during Prohibition. Fireball's father was serving a life sentence in prison. Given Greaves' background as an FBI agent, Fireball did not take to Greaves' presence on the mission very well. He periodically would stare up at Greaves and spit chewing tobacco on the floor of the plane as he assembled various explosives and placed them in a big, Army green pouch.

Accompanying them on the mission was another Yalie; a medical expert named Dr. Elbridge Mace. He had studied the notes the doctors had taken of the alien Bandit while he was in American captivity and was coming along to render any aid as best he could, should the alien be wounded. Mace was fast asleep in the back of the plane. He struck Greaves as a real bon vivant; always looking for a wild adventure. If he hadn't joined the military to fight the war, Mace assumed that the man would've ended up in the Congo as a missionary, living in a hut.

This was his team. The air around them was quiet. They had made it through Naziland and were now moving swiftly to their drop point. Over the radio, they heard the desperate calls from the A20s, which were no longer within view. They weren't going to make it.

"Hey, Captain!" Marks called up to the pilots. "Yes, Captain Marks?" The pilot called back. "Those boys aren't gonna make it. Can you cut that off?" Marks said in a saddened tone. "Yes, sir." The pilot said. Marks looked down at Greaves sternly. "This mission had better be worth their sacrifice."

He cautioned Greaves.

Greaves stared up at Marks and nodded. "It is." He said coldly. None of these men intimidated him. They were a means to an end, in his view.

"We're about an hour out! Get some sleep, boys!" Marks commanded.

He then sat down beside Greaves and glared at him. "This mission had better be everything you say it is, too."

Greaves glowered. "This mission is whatever Washington wants it to be, Captain Marks."

Marks shook his head. *Washington.* He repeated bitterly and leaned back, closing his eyes.

Greaves then noticed Corporal Takeuchi Itijima—Taki—had closed his Bible and sat quietly with his head down, praying. Takeuchi then glanced up at Greaves. "So, you saw it?"

Greaves furrowed his brow. "What?" "The creature." Taki prompted. Greaves said nothing in response, instinctively protecting the information. "It's okay, Lieutenant Greaves. We're all spies here." Taki said reassuringly. Greaves smiled. "Does that help you?" He asked, referring to the Bible. Taki nodded. "Yes, sir. It's gotten me through a lot." "Why'd you join?" Greaves asked. Taki sat back and shrugged. "It was the right thing to do." "Even in spite of what the government did to you?" Greaves prompted. Taki stared intensely at Greaves. "My grandfather was born in Japan. He came here as a man to work on the railroads. He then brought my grandmother over, her parents arranging the marriage." Taki explained. "My father was born here. My mother was born in Japan. My parents had an arranged marriage just like my grandparents." Taki continued recounting. "But my dad and I..." He trailed sadly. *"We're Americans."* He added proudly. "Honestly, sir, it was bullshit what the government did to us." Taki said. Greaves looking sternly at the young man. "But, after Pearl, there was no way I was just going to sit on my hands in that internment camp while my country was under attack." Taki said proudly.

Greaves, who was a ball of blind ambition and power-seeking, could not help but to be moved by the young man. He patted Taki on the shoulder. "Yeah, I've seen the creature." He said nonchalantly. Greaves glanced out the window behind them. The shooting around the plane had stopped. They'd made it through the supposedly impenetrable Naziland air defense zone. "I saw it all that day." He added distantly.

"Did it change you, sir?" Taki asked.

Greaves shrugged. He pointed at the Bible in Taki's hand. "It certainly made me question much of what's in there."

Taki clung to it defensively. "I don't want to see it, then." Greaves smiled. "Corporal, I think the fewer people see this thing, the better." Taki nodded and sat back in his seat. From across Greaves' seat, Sergeant Major O'Shaughnessy spat chewing tobacco on the floor and was cleaning his B.A.R., a long-barreled machine gun that packed quite a wallop. Greaves stared back at the weapons expert. "You've got a problem, Sergeant? Or is there some other reason you've been staring at me since we departed?"

The short but buff sergeant major, nicknamed "Fireball," let out a surly huff. "You Irish?" He asked in clipped, curt manner.

Greaves rolled his eyes. "My mother was Irish."

Fireball chewed more on his tobacco. "I fookin' knew it." He said. "Black Irish." He added, referring to Greaves' thick, black hair.

Greaves regarded the red-haired weapons expert with bemusement. This was not an ordinary military unit. While they all had military ranks, these men were spies first and soldiers a distant second, so the discipline was somewhat lax. Greaves had not served in a military setting in years, so he felt more comfortable here. Greaves was more concerned with the fact that these men were going to ask far too many questions. They'd all been made aware of the details of the operation. But, given the sensitivity and unique nature of their target, Greaves knew that after the mission the government would attempt to mop up any messes that were made from too many people learning about the alien and its technology, all to prevent the public from finding out the truth of what had happened at Cape Girardeau back in '41. Greaves intended to do the mopping, not being mopped up.

"You were a fed before this, though." Fireball said in an accusatory tone. Greaves smirked. "That's right, Sergeant Major." Fireball shook his head in disgust. "Spent your time going after workin' stiffs like my

Old Man!" Greaves stared coldly at Fireball. "I never worked anything related to the Volstead Act."

He said earnestly, referring to the law that had outlawed liquor in the United States for a period of time. "I worked counterintelligence. Y'know? I went after spies." He explained defensively.

"Yeah, we've got former feds in our ranks." Fireball said dismissively. "All of 'em are the same: cockier than God!"

"Okay." Greaves said. "What I'm sayin' is, the sooner we get this mission over with, the better." Fireball said firmly.

Greaves nodded. "Well on that, Sergeant Major, we are in complete agreement." Fireball had finished cleaning his weapon and scoffed. *"Fookin' Feds!"* Dr. Elbridge Mace leaned forward, cutting off the tense conversation between Fireball and Greaves. "So, what condition do you believe the entity will be in when we get to the Nazi facility?"

Greaves stared blankly at the doctor. "Well, it's been in Nazi captivity for more than two years, so..." He trailed, shrugging.

"Yes, but—" Mace began. "I've no idea, Doctor." Greaves said coolly. "I reviewed the notes from the Army docs who initially studied the being—" Mace was cut off again by Greaves. "Then your guess is as good as mine." Greaves said in an annoyed tone. Mace stared at Greaves. "So you can offer me nothing more?" "The medical side of this operation is your business, Dr. Mace." Greaves said coldly. *"Fookin' Feds!"* Fireball huffed. Greaves glared back at Fireball and then returned his gaze to Mace. "You need to be ready for anything." Mace nodded, looking unsure. The fact of the matter was that no one knew for certain how to react or respond to the alien. It was, by definition, an unknown. *"Captain!"* Called out the pilot from the cockpit. Captain Marks remained sitting beside Greaves with his eyes closed and his cap over his eyes. "Yes?" He asked calmly.

"We've got a problem up here!" The pilot shouted, sounding frantic. Captain Marks lifted his cap and looked toward the cockpit, sighing. "What is it?" *"We're surrounded by...something...!"* The pilot said. At that, both Marks and Greaves glanced out the window. Dancing silently around the wings of the plane were bluish-purplish orbs of light. They were fixating on the propeller engines on the transport.

"What is that?!" Marks demanded. *"I don't know, sir!"* The pilot replied. "How far are we from the drop zone?" Greaves asked the pilot. *"Twenty more minutes, at least, sir!"* The pilot replied. Greaves shook his head and stood. As he stood, the engine on Greaves' side of the plane made a sputtering noise and started to deactivate. Greaves glanced over at looked at the cockpit and could see the pilots moving frantically over the controls.

"Okay, we're losing an engine!" The pilot shouted.

Now, Captain Marks was standing and he marched up to the cockpit. "What the Hell is happening?!" He demanded.

Greaves signaled for Taki to stand. When he did, he motioned for Taki to turn around and Greaves began checking Taki's parachute to ensure that it was in working order. Afterward, Greaves turned around and Taki began checking Greaves' chute, too. When they finished checking each other, Taki moved over to Dr. Mace to do the same. Greaves pointed at Fireball who scoffed at him. *"My chute is fine!"* Fireball thundered and began packing his weapons and explosives. *"I don't need your fookin' help!"* He said angrily.

Greaves then marched to the back of the plane and opened the door. *"What're you doing?!"* Captain Marks called after Greaves from the front of the plane. "Captain Marks, this plane isn't going to make it to the drop zone!" Greaves said matter- of-factly. *"We're too far away and too high above the ground for a jump!"* Marks said angrily. Greaves shook his head. "Captain Marks, if we wait any longer, we won't make it!" Marks stared intently at Greaves and saw the seriousness in his face. Marks was clearly thinking about what next to do. After a long while, he nodded and marched back to where Greaves and the rest of the team were. "We're jumping now!" He decreed.

"Roger that, sir! I'm descending to jump altitude!" The pilot said nervously. "Can you boys get back to base safely?" Marks asked the pilot. *"So long as those...foo fighters don't take out the other engine, yes, sir!"* The pilot responded. Marks nodded. "Then the sooner we get off this bird and on the ground, the better!" The

Captain shouted. He then began checking Fireball's parachute and Fireball returned the favor. He then pushed his way to the front of the jump line where Greaves ready to jump. Marks waved Greaves away. "I'm CO of this mission! I'm the first to jump and the last to leave!"

Greaves shrugged and moved behind Marks in the jump line, pushing Fireball a space back, prompting the angry Irishman to let out an animalistic snarl.

"Easy, boy." Greaves said sarcastically to Fireball who scowled at that remark. Greaves glanced up at the ceiling and saw a red light, indicating that they were still too high to jump. When it turned green, they'd be able to jump out of the damaged plane.

"Okay, these things are moving to the other engine!" The pilot screamed. "What, exactly, is going on with the plane?" Taki shouted back. *"Whatever these things are, they're interfering with the plane's power!"* The pilot responded. At that point, the loud whirring sound of the plane's propeller engines dissipated and only the sound of howling wind could be heard. The plane was completely out of power. *"That's it! We're dead in the water!"* The pilot shouted. Marks looked up and saw that the light was still red. "We've gotta go." Greaves urged.

Marks shook his head, pointing at the light. "We're still too high."

Suddenly, a round of explosions erupted all along the plane. The Germans knew they were overhead.

"We've gotta go, *now!*" Greaves shouted at Marks. Without another word, Greaves pushed beyond Marks and dove out of the plane.

"Goddamn it!" Marks shouted. He then turned back to the pilots. "You boys need to bail!" He ordered.

"We're going to try to keep this thing flying until you're all cleared!" The pilot called back.

Marks knew it was a death sentence. He just nodded in understanding and gave the pilots the thumbs up. He glanced up and saw that the light flashed green. "All right, boys, let's go see where Greaves got off to!" Marks then dove out of the plane, into a sea of darkness below that was punctuated by the explosions from the flak that Nazi cannons were lobbing up at the plane. Seconds later, the sky erupted in an explosion as one of the Nazi flak rounds scored a direct hit on the stricken plane, destroying it, and killing the two pilots onboard.

Welcome to Naziland. Marks thought angrily to himself.

Walther Brünow stood in the forest which led into Peenemunde. He and his group of heavily armed friends waited anxiously for their American contacts to arrive. They were already two hours overdue. Ordinarily, he'd have ordered his team to disband and return home before they were discovered by the twitchy Nazi patrol that circled the secret Nazi proving ground in northern Germany, along the Baltic Sea. A V-2 Rocket had already streaked into the sky earlier that evening, undoubtedly heading toward Britain. Another blot on the Nazi's long record of tyranny and terror that Walther and his fellow members of the Germany Catholic resistance movement knew would stain Germany and her people for generations unless Hitler and his goons were stopped. Since it was the Americans—the OSS, no less—Walther had opted to risk his team and stay longer.

A dock worker by trade, Walther had commanded much respect among the local population in Peenemunde. He was 55 and his family had long been involved in local politics. Walther had joined the German resistance when the Nazis started to tightly regulate the local Catholic churches and when the Gestapo started terrorizing the members of the local unions, whom they accused of being communist spies (they were not. Their deep Catholicism forbade beliefs in Marxism). Walther's friends comprised the rest of his resistance cell. There was Alois, the local butcher whose oldest son had been killed fighting Hitler's unjust war in the East, against the Soviets. Alois crouched in the foliage below where Walther had hunkered down, watching for unwanted Nazi activity beyond. Alois was 47, balding, and extraordinarily thin and tall—something that made Walther and his friends laugh, as he sold the best salted meats in the area at his shop. Like the rest of the group, Alois was deeply Catholic and hated the Nazis more than any of them. Walther knew that Alois would stay in the forest waiting for the American commandos until Hell froze over if it was necessary.

Gunther Weiss was a bear of a man. Like Walther, Gunther worked at the docks. He had been in the Wehrmacht and had partaken in the invasion of France two years prior. But, he was wounded and was sent back home. When he returned home, Gunther became disenchanted by Nazi policies toward the Catholic church and joined the resistance cell. Walther's group was massive and was part of a larger pan-German Catholic resistance front led by the Austrian priest Heinrich Maier and his organization, the Austrian Committee of Liberation, was the most significant resistance front within Germany. It was their extensive resistance movement that had amassed critical intelligence on Nazi secret weapons facilities and offloaded those plans to OSS and British intelligence over the years.

There were other members of Walther's resistance cell scattered throughout the forest, many of them former Wehrmacht members, like Gunther. All of them were united in their Catholicism and their fear that the Nazis were coming to destroy the Church. There were about 30 heavily armed men waiting for Walther's order to attack. Gunther, however, looked despondent.

"They are not coming, Walther." Gunther said in German. Walther shook his head. "They will come." Gunther sighed. "My friend, you heard about the air raid last night. All of the American planes were destroyed." Walther stared down at the gigantic Gunther. "If you wish to leave, you may at any point,

Gunther." Gunther's eyes widened. "I am no coward!" He seethed.

Walther smiled at his friend and patted him on the shoulder. "I swear that is not what I meant."

Gunther nodded.

"You have sacrificed much over these years. And if you believe your talents are not needed here today then you may go." Walther said reassuringly.

Gunther shook his head. "If we are discovered—"

Walther smiled. "If we are discovered, the resistance movement will go on. God is on our side."

Suddenly, to Walther's left was a loud rustling in the bushes followed by Alois, who was now pointing his machine gun toward the rustling bushes, going, *"Psst!"*

Walther and Gunther both raised their weapons and readied for a shootout with a Nazi patrol. Instead, it was US Army Captain Marks. Walther beamed. He had met Captain Marks once, while Marks was exfiltrating a Jewish physicist who had been taken to Peenemunde to be worked to death in the mines there.

"Hello, my friend!" Marks whispered in German to Walther.

Walther lowered his weapon and trundled down the hill, embracing the American. "It is good to see you again!"

Marks nodded, looking tired and dirty from what Walther assumed was a rough night of marching and evading Nazi patrols.

"Are you all here?" Walther asked.

Marks said, "Yes." He then stepped aside and held back some bushes, revealing his OSS team. They, too, looked haggard. "Minus one." Marks said sadly. "Our medical officer was killed during the jump." He explained in German, shaking his head as he remembered finding the doctor's corpse tangled in its parachute and wrapped around a tree.

"We heard about the battle in the sky." Walther said. Marks nodded. "We almost did not survive it." Gunther then peeked through the bushes. "This is your entire team?" He asked in broken

English. Marks nodded again. He then began introducing them one at a time. "That's Corporal

Takeuchi Itijima, our communications officer—we call him Taki—that's Sergeant Major O'Shaughnessy, our weapons expert—" The massive Gunther locked eyes with the short but muscular O'Shaughnessy, and the two men nodded at each other in respect. "—We call him "Fireball," for obvious reasons." Marks paused and then stared at Greaves. "And that's Lieutenant Patrick Greaves." He said dispassionately. Marks then leaned in and said, "He's the new guy."

Greaves glowered and marched through the foliage. "So, are we going to stand around here and have coffee hour or are we going to get this show on the road?"

Marks grimaced at Greaves' forwardness. Walther looked taken aback. "Does he speak German?" Walther asked Marks in German. Marks shook his head. "No." Greaves smirked and, in perfect German, he said, "Yes, of course I speak German!" Marks' eyes widened. "I didn't—" Greaves shrugged. "Need to know." He chastised Marks in English. "That would've been—" Marks began. "Irrelevant." Greaves said coldly.

Marks stared in astonishment at Greaves. *Irrelevant?!* He wondered angrily to himself. *For a mission that takes us into the heart of Germany?!*

Greaves got in Marks' face. "Let's get one thing clear here, Captain: I don't report to you!"

"Like Hell you don't!" Marks hissed.

Greaves shook his head. "No, I don't. I report to Washington. This mission and its prioritization is unlike anything you and your team have ever worked, understand?"

Marks looked angry and said nothing.

"So, yes, you are in charge of the mission on the ground here, but I am the guy the White House personally appointed to take care of this matter." Greaves said, reminding them of the fact that he personally briefed the president. "Now, we're on the clock. The sooner we get this thing over with, the better."

"Why so few of you?" Gunther asked in German. "Because this is all that Washington could spare." Greaves said cryptically. "How many men do you have out here?" Marks asked Walther, tabling his greater issues with the arrogant and cold Greaves. "Twenty." Walther replied.

Greaves nodded. "The uniforms?"

Walther smiled and glanced over at Alois. "Oh, do we have the uniforms..." He trailed and then he gave Captain Marks a playful tap. "Just like last time." He said with a large grin on his face, referring to the previous time they infiltrated Peenemunde together. Of course, this was slightly different. They did not go on base, which was located on an island just across from where the men were currently standing. Back then, to liberate the Jewish physicist, they went to a holding area adjacent from the island. Boats moved the slave laborers and scientists who worked on the base to and from their homes nearby.

Alois pulled up a rucksack and unfurled it, revealing a gray and white Nazi officer's uniform.

"Papers?" Marks inquired, knowing that they'd need valid identification to enter the heavily fortified island facility. Walther nodded nonchalantly. "Taken care of, my friend."

Marks chuckled and nodded happily at the German resistance fighter. "Way to go, Walther!"

"And the bastards never plugged the gaps in their security from the last time you joined us!" Walther said excitedly.

Marks furrowed his brow. "That doesn't sound like the Nazis..." "These are very arrogant people." Gunther huffed knowingly. Marks thought about it for a moment. "So, it's the same play from before, then?" He asked, sounding more like the Yale football quarterback than a spy. "What about the timing of this thing?" Greaves inquired, as he had taken Walther's previous position just below the dirt mount that gave him unobstructed views of both the Nazi patrol area and the bay that led to the island where Peenemunde's proving grounds were located. In the distance, the echoes of officious—almost robotic—Nazi officers could be heard issuing edicts and announcements over the island base's loudspeaker system echoed throughout the area.

Walther looked over at Greaves uneasily. "There are some boats that are kept by the living quarters to allow for the soldiers to come and go as they need to. We will take one of those boats over to the island." He explained.

"No one will ask any questions?" Greaves inquired skeptically. "Our papers will get us onto the base, Mr. Greaves." Alois said confidently. "But we have to time this operation well." Walther cautioned. "They do their experiments with Die Glocke and other exotic propulsion technologies around sundown." He explained. Greaves looked confused. "What does that matter?" "Your visitors are brought from their confinement underground to the surface where they are made to control the vehicles." Alois said. Greaves scoffed. "I thought we were retrieving these things from their holding area underground." Walther laughed. "If we go down below, we will never get out of there alive." "The whole point of this operation is subtlety." Greaves complained. "There's nothing subtle about walking up to the most secure Nazi military facility in the whole Reich and plucking the package right from in front of the Nazi's eyes!" He exclaimed, confused as to how such a silly plan could have been hatched.

"We can distract them long enough to allow for you to escape." Walther said reassuringly.

Marks nodded. "Plus, Taki here is going to call into Bomber Command and the Brits are going to blitz the bejesus of this whole area tonight."

Greaves knew that part of their plan entailed using the cover of an Allied air raid to mask their escape. "Yes, but the plan of us exfiltrating with the visitor by sea only works if we take him from his cell, without anyone noticing."

"Unfortunately, we can't get down there." Walther said. "These identification papers are good but they only get us on the island. They don't get us underneath it." He explained in an annoyed tone, upset that he was having to explain himself repeatedly to the obnoxious American spy.

"It's fine." Marks said sternly, wanting to end the conversation before they offended the German resistance members they needed to survive this ordeal.

Greaves shook his head. This was quickly becoming a suicide mission. "Great planning: we've got a perfect way in...and no way out!" He quipped sarcastically.

Marks grabbed a rucksack with a Nazi uniform in it and shoved it into Greaves' hands. "Just get this on and let's get ready!" The Ivy League officer airily commanded. Nothing fazed this man, even an apparent suicide mission.

Greaves scoffed and began doing as he was told. As he disrobed and placed on the Nazi officer's uniform, he fixated on something that Walther had said, unsure if it was just a language barrier. "You keep referring to the visitor in plural sense..." Greaves trailed.

Walther, who was also donning a Nazi uniform nodded. "Yes." "Why?" Marks interjected. Walther looked confused. "There are two of them in there." He said. Greaves and Marks exchanged shocked glances.

"I thought all the other ones died in the Cape Girardeau crash." Marks said, starting to think that Greaves was lying about key aspects of this mission.

"They were!" Greaves shot back defensively.

"One of them is not from America." Walther whispered. "One of them has been here for almost ten years. It was captured alive in the Black Forest." He concluded.

"Can you make it out with two of them?" Marks asked.

Greaves nodded. "They're tiny. It shouldn't matter if there were one or ten of them." But Greaves began worrying that maybe the aliens were helping the Nazis.

For his part, Marks' mind was racing. He did not want to give Greaves any credit. But, the G-Man wasn't wrong. This was quickly devolving into a suicide mission and Marks needed to quickly figure out a better escape plan than they currently had.

"We should hold here until the sun starts to go down. How much longer until that happens?" Marks inquired.

"One more hour." Gunther responded. Marks nodded. "Okay, guys, we hold here for an hour. Then we move." Greaves shook his head. Marks walked over to Taki. "Report into command and tell them to get ready to unleash

Hell over these skies." He said. Taki nodded. "Yes, sir."

Greaves was upset. He did not sign up to die.

CHAPTER FIFTEEN: ESCAPE FROM PEENEMUNDE

Hans Kammler stood proudly in the back of the concrete testing site. Since his interaction with the gray aliens, everything had started falling into place. Antigravity vehicles that his team had created over a year ago based on alien designs finally began working and *Die Glocke* had enjoyed some marginal if still interesting gains in its testing. Intelligence reported a large movement of Allied bombers coming from Britain that would be over Peenemunde shortly. Kammler intended for the grays to finally prove their worth and deploy the silent, antigravity orbs to swarm the incoming bombers. An individual plane proved no match for these systems that disrupted the electronics on Allied bombers. Yet, there were usually so many bombers that the Allies sent against German targets that they couldn't all be stopped. Kammler expected things tonight to be different.

Werner von Braun wore an elegant suit. The mood in Peenemunde had shifted since the advanced technology that the aliens had been working on had started functioning properly. Of course, there were still detractors. Not all scientists, such as Heisenberg, at the facility were sanguine about their chances. There were anti-Nazi resistors throughout the land. And as the war had ground on with a decreasing chance of victory, many more Germans were beginning to sympathize and join the ranks of the resistance. Kammler himself had become adept at playing both ends against the middle. Shortly before the tests had begun going well, Kammler had contemplated reaching out to Western intelligence.

He backed away from those thoughts once things started going better in recent weeks. Although, Kammler still could not shake the feeling that they may have been too-little-too-late. Unlike some of the others who questioned Hitler's Final Victory, though, Kammler was a true believer which is why he ultimately resisted the urge to betray the Reich. Heisenberg stood shaking his head as he watched two Nazi guards escorting the tiny gray beings to the stationary *Die Glocke*. His stomach churned at the sight of such monstrosity. The older gray being, looking ragged and weaker than he has ever looked, was placed gently into the craft while the Nazi guards took the seemingly helpless tinier alien, the one that the American president had nicknamed "Bandit," and stood in a clearing in direct line of sight from the experimental vehicle. The guards were unarmed and all metal had been removed from their uniforms, making them look somewhat silly, in Heisenberg's opinion. Of course, Heisenberg was keenly aware that any metal or energy device could be fashioned into a weapon by the small creature once known as Bandit.

One of the Nazi guards lifted the tiny being off the ground while the other stood with his right hand clasped tightly around the creature's throat. The implication was clear: if the older gray being, known to the Germans as "Hansel," did not comply with Kammler's demands, then Kammler would order Bandit to be strangled to death in front of the alien. The two guards that Kammler had selected to do this task, Heisenberg knew, were among the most sadistic troops that Kammler had at their disposal. Even if Hansel did try to stop them by deploying *Die Glocke*'s technology against them, Heisenberg assessed that the guards would die trying to murder the tiny creature rather than risk Hansel freeing Bandit from their grasp.

Heisenberg nervously checked his watch, glancing around to see if he could spot the German resistance members he had made contact with. He knew they were coming for these beings. He did not know, however, who they were.

"You are nervous, Dr. Heisenberg?" Kammler inquired in an almost teasing tone.

Heisenberg said nothing but looked on in horror as he saw the aliens loaded into the *Die Glocke*. "This could kill them, Obergruppenführer." Kammler chuckled. "These creatures are almost Aryan in their stamina." Heisenberg shook his head. "Be thankful, Doctor, that you are necessary for the Reich." Kammler said, dropping all pretense of enjoyment. "For without that mind of yours, a bullet would have been delivered to the back of your skull long ago!"

Heisenberg glared back at Kammler, unafraid of the threats. "A bullet awaits for all of us. Sooner than we realize, Obersgruppenführer."

Kammler smirked. "Not so long as these weapons exist, I think."

At that Heisenberg let out a bellowing laugh. "What have these weapons done? The Allies still blitz us daily! And Dresden…" He trailed bitterly, thinking of the wanton destruction visited upon the great, historic city along the Elbe River. All of which could have been avoided had Berlin sued for peace in a war they were clearly losing.

Kammler was indifferent. "A necessary sacrifice." He stated matter-of-factly as he watched the aliens be loaded into *Die Glocke.* "From the fire and ashes a newer, better Germany will be reborn. Indeed, it is almost Wagnerian in its undertone!" Kammler enthused.

Heisenberg looked away in disgust. "Look around you, sir! This is not the beginning of something wonderful. This is the tragic end of our nation!"

Kammler was enraged. "I've had enough of you, Doctor! If you've nothing more to add to this demonstration, then you are dismissed!" He shouted angrily.

Heisenberg glanced back at von Braun who stared nervously, worried that the legendary scientist might get himself shot. After a long moment, Heisenberg acquiesced and marched out of the testing area. While Heisenberg departed, Kammler watched what he believed was the misguided scientist leave. When Heisenberg entered his car and was driven away, Kammler returned his attention to *Die Glocke.* A low, but growing louder, hum of energy emanated from below and around them as *Die Glocke* was powered up by Peenemunde's massive power generators (which drew on power from the nearby town).

"Powering up now!" Von Braun announced.

Kammler smiled widely. He envisioned himself being awarded an Iron Cross and possibly being made the centerpiece of the next great Leni Reifenstahl film; celebrated all over the Reich for having vanquished the Allied invaders and giving their country a renewed lease on life and honor. With the sun having recently set, Kammler knew the Allied bombers were incoming. They rarely attacked this part of Germany because it was so heavily fortified, but Kammler reasoned that they were figuring out that new weapons were being devised at this location, and the Allies wanted to try to slow their progress down.

The sound of energy roared around them as *Die Glocke* whirred to life before them. From around *Die Glocke,* multiple bluish-purplish electromagnetic, antigravity orbs appeared. These would be the weapons they deployed against the incoming Allied planes—and this time, Kammler believed the orbs would do their job and destroy all the Allied bombers.

Die Glocke spun wildly as the chains holding it down strained under the increased stress. Kammler nodded excitedly, expecting this test to go far differently than the previous ones had. He glanced over at the small creature whose life hung in the balance before the madly spinning *Die Glocke.* All was well in Kammler's world. The weak were kept in their place by the strong.

Air raid sirens began wailing all around them.

Kammler's aid, Nazi SS Colonel Ernst Richter marched up behind Kammler and von Braun with a worried look on his face. For his part, von Braun was moving away from *Die Glocke* and heading toward a concrete bunker nearby where he could hide from any possible bombs, fearing that the test site where *Die Glocke* was powered up was an obvious target for Allied bombs. Kammler stood tall, staring intently at the wildly swinging *Die Glocke.* The two soldiers holding Bandit hostage did not move either. They were fanatics of the sort that Kammler associated with: they would not be moved by the threat of Allied bombing.

"Sir, Allied bombers are within striking distance of this location." Richter said, motioning for Kammler to follow him.

Kammler ignored his aid and took two steps forward.

A look of fear flashed across Richter's face. He stepped forward, directly behind Kammler. "Obersgruppenführer?" He prompted.

Kammler was ensconced in the strange, alien beauty of *Die Glocke* as it spun around before him, with the electromagnetic, antigravity orbs dancing around it. He was transfixed on the otherworldly display before him. "Tell me, Colonel," Kammler began, as if in a trance, "Are *you* an ardent National Socialist?"

Richter said nothing, contemplating his next words carefully. Of course, he was. But he did not possess a death wish. "Y-yes, Obersgruppenführer!"

Kammler nodded slowly. "And are *you* aware of how Wotan received his wisdom and strength?" The mad Nazi leader asked, referring to the character of Wotan from Wagner's *The Ring Cycle* opera, one of Wagner's most famous pieces.

Richter shook his head.

Kammler glanced back madly. "Wotan plucked out one of his eyes to receive his wisdom!" The hum of the energy was so great that even the blaring air raid sirens could not be heard. The moment that Kammler finished that sentence, though, a series of explosions erupted from behind Kammler.

"*The Allied bombs!*" Von Braun gasped as he dove into the nearby concrete bunker.

Kammler knew better than that. The explosion came from behind the island, where the German mainland was located. The bombers were coming in from across the sea, in front of them. "*Sabotage!*" Kammler screamed madly as all the power on the island instantly shut down. Instantly, the load roaring and manic maneuvering of *Die Glocke* was replaced by an eerie silence that was only punctuated by the blaring klaxons of the air raid sirens.

Darkness descended on the proving ground, since someone had obliterated the massive power generator that powered the entire facility. Kammler composed himself and was reassured by the fact that the backups would kick on soon. Once they did, Hansel would be able to continue his mission of defense. Approaching from the distance, Kammler could hear the hum of Allied bombers moving closer. Even if the backup generator activated, *Die Glocke* would not have time to power itself and launch the electromagnetic antigravity orbs—what the Allies called "Foo Fighters."

Kammler turned to his aid, Richter. "Get word to the airfield to deploy conventional air defenses! *Die Glocke* will be delayed!"

Richtie snapped a salute and then went running off to relay Kammler's orders.

Immediately, power was restored as the sound of the backup generator erupted from across the testing facility. Kammler grinned proudly at the efficiency with which his operation performed under immense pressure. However, almost as quickly as the power was restored the backup generator erupted in a dazzling explosion and power shut down yet again.

"*NO!*" Kammler screamed. He pivoted to where his two loyal guards were holding the younger gray alien, Bandit, in place. Through the darkness, Kammler spied what appeared to be two officers approaching the guards, with weapons in hand. No one was supposed to approach the creature with weapons or any form of metal on their persons. Kammler reached out as if signaling for the two officers, whom Kammler did not recognize but saw that one was a colonel and the other a major, to stop approaching the creature, whose eyes glowed white in the darkness.

Before Kammler could react, the sky above him exploded in a rage as the air defense guns of the base roared to life. Flares illuminated the dark skies above, revealing innumerable Allied bombers flying overhead. The flak cannons pulsed to life and sent their devastating payloads flying desperately up toward the Allied bombers. Kammler gritted his teeth. The screeching of four *Messerschmitt Me262* fighter jets came from the runway behind Kammler's location. These were experimental fighter jets, the first of their kind, that could fly 100 miles faster than the fastest Allied propeller-driven aircraft. Kammler did not have enough of these jet fighters to win the war yet. But, he had a squadron that could adequately defend the base in a pinch—and Kammler was in a very serious pinch.

"*You there!*" Kammler screamed at the unknown officers who were almost eye-to-eye with his two guards holding Bandit hostage. "*Stand back!*" He commanded.

The officers either could not hear Kammler or ignored him. *"STAND BACK!"* Kammler screamed again. The larger officer, whose uniform Kammler could tell the closer he got, did not fit him properly simply glanced back nonchalantly at the approaching Kammler. The two guards holding the creature hostage looked confused. The flashes of an air battle raging in the skies above the facility made Kammler think that the scene would make for a magnificent painting to hang in his study. His fantasies were cut short when the officer with a colonel's rank shot the two preoccupied guards in the head and the larger officer, the one wearing the ill-fitting uniform with a major's insignia on it, placed a black, burlap bag over the alien.

Without hesitation, Kammler pulled out his Lugar pistol and began firing madly. *"Saboteurs!"* He screamed in German, hoping that some of his troops, all of whom were preoccupied with the slap-dash defense of Peenemunde, would hear him.

The larger man in the poorly tailored major's uniform was unfazed by Kammler's mad firing at them. He turned around, revealing a machine gun and fired a burst. It missed, though it did kick up dirt from the ground in front of Kammler, which landed in his eye. Kammler fired again, knowing that the alien they were kidnapping was his only chance to make the machines his team had created here work. Kammler settled himself and took aim at the larger man who was running behind the strange Nazi colonel carrying Bandit in a burlap sack. One shot was fired by the cool as a cucumber Kammler. That one shot landed perfectly in the square of the larger man's back. He dropped without another word.

Kammler rejoiced momentarily and then took aim at the other man carrying Bandit. Right as he went to squeeze trigger, the pistol jammed. Kammler's eyes widened. The Lugar was one of the most reliable handguns in the world. It'd never jammed on Kammler before. He moved it aside and stared at it in confusion. He then looked up and saw the door to *Die Glocke* open and Hansel was standing, waving his arms in a manner that Kammler immediately understood meant that he was using his telekinesis to jam the weapon.

"YOU!" Kammler screamed accusatorily at the older, dying alien. He threw the gun aside and went charging toward *Die Glocke.* When he got within arm's length of Hansel, though, he could tell that the craft was powered up. This should have been impossible as the craft required a massive charge from the facility's power grid which was presently deactivated, thanks to the saboteurs who had kidnapped Bandit. Kammler ignored the fact that *Die Glocke* was fully operational and went to grab the tiny Hansel from the open hatchway. When he reached inside the craft an electric hissing emanated from the craft which made Kammler feel as though all his nerves were on fire and sent him flying many feet back from where he had come from.

Disoriented and in pain, Kammler composed himself and stood up again, marveling at the power that Hansel was exhibiting and in shock as he saw *Die Glocke* lift itself slowly into the air, its metal chains breaking away effortlessly as Hansel clearly navigated the craft into the sky. As Kammler watched in anger and shock at the image of his prized wonder weapon leaving his control, he heard the familiar click of his Lugar and turned to see another Nazi officer holding it to his head.

"Obersgruppenführer," the officer said knowingly, but Kammler did not recognize the man.

Kammler stared at the man's face for a long while and immediately recognized him from intelligence reports. The man was a top-ranking FBI counterintelligence operative who had helped to dismantle Fritz Duquesne's spy ring in the United States and had wreaked havoc on Nazi spy operations in South America. "Patrick Greaves!" Kammler gasped.

Greaves was taken aback. He simply stared and raised the Lugar coldly in Kammler's face.

Kammler pretended to be more scared than he was. He winced at the sight of the pistol being raised in his face. Kammler winced. *"Oh God! DON'T SHOOT ME!"* Kammler screamed, managing to evoke some tears from his eyes.

Greaves grimaced, disgusted by this man's cowardice. "Don't you know who I am?" Kammler demanded, crying.

Greaves shook his head. "I'm your source!" Kammler screamed. Greaves looked around, confused. "What?" "Who do you think gave the resistance the information, the uniforms, the papers they needed to get in here?" Kammler screamed in perfect English. Greaves was alone, so he could not confirm or disconfirm what Kammler was saying. "I'm the resistance's source! If you kill me, you're going to destroy the resistance!"

Kammler said desperately. Greaves raised the pistol again. "I could be of use to you and your agency, too!" Kammler screamed, raising his hands frantically. Greaves put the pistol down. "How?" Kammler looked around, hoping that his troops would arrive. He was annoyed when he saw that no one was coming. They were all too distracted with the battle overhead. "I...I...Everyone other than the Fuhrer knows that this war is lost!" Kammler screamed. "That your army will be here soon, whether it's this week or next year, they will be here!" He continued.

"And?" Greaves said, getting worried that he was about to be left behind by the rescue team.

"I have access to sophisticated technology that your country could use in their pending war with the Reds." Kammler said enticingly.

Greaves recoiled. Greaves watched with amazement as the bell-shaped Nazi craft moved toward where Bandit and the resistance members had taken him. He smirked. "It looks like I already have your sophisticated technology."

Kammler closed his eyes. "That's not all there is here! If you're not careful, you'll destroy it and it won't be of use to anyone!" He shouted frantically.

Greaves thought about it for a second, remembering the strange airplanes he saw rocketing from the runway behind them. "Okay." Greaves said.

"Remember me, Agent Greaves. I can be your country's man on the inside. And when the time is right, I can preserve these wonder weapons and give them to your country...in exchange for my freedom, of course!" Kammler negotiated.

There was silence. He opened his eyes, realizing that Greaves had run off into the night. On the ground before him, though, Greaves had left a business card with the FBI logo on it. The card had Greaves' personal contact information. Realizing that he was free and alive, Kammler laughed giddily. He stood and went running toward where his troops would be, pocketing the business card as he ran away.

Greaves ran at full speed to catch up with Walther, running past Gunther's dead body in the field where Kammler had shot him in the back. Ahead of Greaves was the bell-shaped *Die Glocke,* which was clearly chasing Bandit and Walther. Greaves did not know if the craft was a threat or not. To his right, he saw that Walther had run down some concrete stairs that led to the docks beyond. Gunshots erupted from down there and Greaves feared the worst: that Bandit had been killed. He quickened his pace.

Greaves ran down the stairs to see that Walther had been shot dead and the burlap bag with Bandit in it had been opened and Bandit was wandering around aimlessly as six Nazi guards ran toward him. Greaves' eyes widened. He took aim with Kammler's pistol and fired at the approaching Nazis. He took two of them down, but the other Nazis managed to take cover and begin firing at Greaves' position at the top of the stairs. Greaves frantically dove down from the stairs, landing in the grassy knoll beyond.

Greaves stood and charged toward Bandit. "Get down!" He screamed at Bandit, not sure if the creature could even understand him. Bullets bounced on the ground around him, but Greaves knew that this being was his entire mission. But Greaves was pinned down. He dove down to the ground as the bullets from the Nazi bullets came precariously close to hitting him.

Just when Greaves thought all was lost, from above them where Greaves had just come from, Taki and Fireball appeared and took aim at the Nazi guards, firing and killing them. Greaves locked eyes with Fireball who scowled at him and then Greaves went charging toward Bandit as Fireball and Taki ran down the stairs to join Greaves.

"What the fook is that thing?!" Fireball demanded when he saw Bandit wandering around.

Greaves grimaced. "It's classified!"

Fireball raised his hands defensively. "Yeah, everything we fookin' do is classified! But that thing is..."

Taki knelt down beside the small creature. "Special." He said, smiling.

Greaves was annoyed and knew they did have much time to escape. Plus, even though he could no longer see the strange, Nazi bell-shaped craft, Greaves suspected it was nearby. "Wonderful. Put it in the bag and forget you ever saw it." Greaves said threateningly.

"Get a load of this guy!" Fireball quipped. He then looked around. "Where's the fookin' Captain?!" He demanded.

Greaves was silent as he realized that Marks was not with them. He shook his head. "Gone, obviously." He said coldly.

"No way! We don't leave him behind!" Fireball screamed. Taki had finished putting Bandit back inside the burlap bag. "If you want go find him, have at it! But we're leaving with the package!" Greaves said firmly. "You cold sonofabitch!" Fireball shouted. "We don't even know where he is." Greaves said coldly. "Weren't you with him?!" Fireball demanded. Greaves shook his head. "We got separated!" "Then lets go back to where you got separated!" Fireball insisted. Greaves got a look of mania on his face. "No." He said firmly. "We're going. Taki, let's move!" Taki paused, carefully slinging the burlap bag around his shoulder and staring at Greaves.

"Uh, sir..." Taki began uncomfortably. "You too?" Greaves prompted, holding back rage at the insubordination. "Understand: the president has given me a direct order!" Greaves shouted. "That's who we're doing this for! Not for General Donovan. Not for Director Hoover. For the president!" Greaves urged.

"Yeah, fook this Fed!" Fireball huffed and turned around to go back up the stairs.

Taki took one step forward, passing a shocked Greaves. When Greaves realized they were taking Bandit with them, he instinctively raised the Lugar he had taken from Kammler, pointed it at Fireball's head and killed him. Without hesitation, he moved the pistol's aim down to a stunned Taki and killed the young corporal as well. When Taki fell to the ground, the burlap bag dropped and opened again, revealing Bandit who stared blankly at Greaves—almost as if he were accusing Greaves of the murders he had just committed. Greaves returned the pistol to his belt, knelt beside Bandit, and tied the sack around him so as not to see the alien being. He then slung the sack around his back and began jogging down the pier to the fast boat that he and the team had taken onto the island.

Greaves was stopped dead-in-his-tracks when he saw a bloodied and wounded Captain Marks standing on the boat, staring coldly at him, his machine gun pointed at Greaves. The captain had survived! Too bad he had not made himself known to Greaves, Fireball, and Taki, because Greaves could have avoided the bloodshed and heartache he had just subjected his two teammates to.

"You treacherous bastard!" Marks hissed, clamoring off the boat and pointing his gun at Greaves' chest.

Undaunted, Greaves stared coldly back at Marks. "We don't have time for this!"

"Like Hell we do!" Marks shouted bitterly, as blood poured from where had been shot in the leg and the left arm. Blood pooled from a large gash across his forehead, too.

"I was under orders." Greaves said coldly. *"To kill my men?!"* Marks screamed madly. Greaves nodded once. "To tie up any loose ends." Marks' eyebrows raised in shock. "From the president?!" Greaves said nothing. Of course, FDR had issued no such order to Greaves. Greaves was making it all up to justify his panicked murders of Fireball and Taki. The wayward agent knew, though, that Marks wasn't buying it. He could sense that his time was coming to a quick close. He braced himself for the barrage of bullets that was about to rip through his chest. Just when Marks was about to pull the trigger, though, a blinding light shone down from above Greaves. It was the bell-shaped Nazi craft.

Oh no! Greaves thought to himself, worried that he was being captured by Nazis. Marks fired a burst from his machine gun, but an invisible force deflected the bullets. One of those bullets ricocheted back at Marks and blasted open his head. Greaves grimaced at the bloody sight. He clung desperately to the burlap bag, assuming that the being inside of it would be his only bargaining chip.

To Greaves' surprise, he was soon levitating off the ground and being pulled inside the strange craft. *This is it!* He thought desperately to himself, a sense of defeat consuming him.

When Patrick Greaves awoke, he was in a windowless hospital room. Both General "Wild Bill" Donovan and FBI Director J. Edgar Hoover stood over him with grim looks on their face. Greaves was sore everywhere and confused. A bright light shone over Greaves and an attractive nurse finished checking on him. Greaves felt as though he had the worst hangover in history.

"What happened?" Greaves moaned. "That was precisely my question, Agent Greaves." Donovan said sternly. Greaves looked bewildered. The entire ordeal surrounding that creature was beyond confusing to him. "I—" Hoover cut his agent off. Scowling, he said, "Whatever you did, you lost them!" He hissed bitterly. Greaves stammered. "Who?"

"The creature!" Hoover prompted angrily.

"How?!" Greaves demanded. "Is this some kind of a...Nazi trick?!" He asked, as the last thing he remembered was being taken inside the strange, experimental Nazi craft.

"What?!" Hoover demanded indignantly.

Donovan regarded the agent with suspicion and then leaned into Hoover. "He may have suffered a mental break."

Hoover was unconvinced. "Not likely."

"You mean to tell us, you remember nothing of what happened out there?" Donovan asked skeptically.

Greaves collected himself, shifting uncomfortably in the hospital bed. "I remember..." He saw the faces of Fireball, Taki, and Marks when he closed his eyes, prompting him to shift uncomfortably yet again. "My whole team was killed." He said.

Donovan nodded. "Yes." He said, sadly.

Greaves stared intently at Donovan, trying to determine if they knew he had murdered his own team. When they said nothing, he continued. "I encountered the commander of the Peenemunde facility." He wheezed.

Hoover's right eyebrow cocked up in interest. "And?" He prompted.

Greaves shook his head dismissively. "He recognized me from my work on the Duquesne spy ring."

"Yes, you're quite the celebrity." Hoover quipped sarcastically.

Greaves shook his head, ignoring his nominal boss' sarcasm. "No, Director Hoover, he claimed he was the inside source for the Austrian resistance."

Donovan then moved himself between Hoover and the delirious Greaves. "That's not right. I know who their source is inside Peenemunde." Donovan said cryptically.

Hoover was annoyed. He wanted to know who it was but he knew that directly asking about it would make him appear weak and give Donovan the ability to deny Hoover access to this information. So, Hoover kept his mouth closed and remained standing with his arms crossed.

Greaves rolled his eyes. "Well, General, he offered his services to us—directly." He explained. "Kammler. Hans Kammler was his name." Greaves said, vaguely remembering the ordeal at the test site.

Hoover was annoyed. "That's all well-and-good, but I want to know what the Hell happened to the creature!"

Greaves shook his head. "I had him!" He said defensively. "He was in a burlap bag around my back..."

"Well, he's gone, son." Donovan murmured. Greaves grimaced. "There was a device..." Hoover and Donovan exchanged knowing glances. "Go on." Hoover demanded.

"It was a Nazi...craft of some sort or another..." Greaves trailed, trying to remember. "It flew over me...shone a light down on me when I was standing on the docks, trying to make it to our escape boat, as per our plans..." Greaves again trailed, trying not to remember the image of Captain Marks' head being blown off by ricocheting bullets that were initially intended to kill Greaves for his murder of Marks' OSS team.

"Was it all bell-shaped craft?" Donovan inquired. Greaves' eyes widened in shock. "Yes, sir!" Hoover looked enraged. Greaves shook his head. "I remember it did something to me..." Donovan leaned in. "Like what?"

Greaves looked confounded. "I-I don't remember!" "Oh, come on, man!" Hoover shouted angrily. Greaves looked innocently at Hoover. "What is it, Director Hoover?" "Three days ago, that thing appeared at the facility in Lynn, Massachusetts, where we had moved the alien craft from Cape Girardeau for study..." Hoover trailed. "Within seconds after it appeared, both the Nazi vehicle and the Cape Girardeau craft were gone!" Hoover explained, his face turning red with anger. He moved closer to the hospital bed. "And in their place, in that hangar, *was you!*" Hoover accused.

Greaves' heart raced. He understood that he was being accused of treason. "I didn't give the Nazis anything!" He shouted defensively.

"Well they got everything!" Hoover shouted. "I'm not a traitor, sir!" Greaves screamed helplessly. Donovan bit his lower lip, clearly torn between what Hoover was saying and what

Greaves was saying in defense of himself. He glanced back at Hoover. "What about the device?" Hoover shot Donovan and angry look. "Wh-what device?" Greaves insisted. "Why would you bring that up here?" Hoover thundered.

"When you were...delivered to the hangar in Massachusetts, you had a device in your hand..." Donovan trailed.

Greaves was desperate. "What device?!" He demanded.

"It was identical to the one that the creature built for the president when it was in our custody back in '41." Donovan explained. He pulled it out from his pocket. It was in a small, airtight container.

As soon as Greaves saw the device, he went pale. Memories from being on the bell- shaped craft came flooding back to him, as if a door had been opened. He stared as if in a trance and said, "It is a message for the president." He said cryptically.

"Saying what?" Hoover demanded. Greaves remained in his trance. "They're coming here." "Who's coming here? The alien?" Donovan asked, confused.

Greaves shook his head, remaining in the trance. "The creatures who destroyed the alien's home." He whispered, fear creeping into his voice.

Hoover looked skeptical. "Oh, come on!" He huffed.

"It's for the president's eyes only." Greaves whispered. He then nodded. "But they're coming here—sooner or later." Greaves said firmly. He then looked squarely into Donovan's eyes and said knowingly, "And we've got to be ready."

Hoover let out a doubtful sigh. "Well, thanks to you, Greaves, the only technology that might have helped get us ready was taken when you came back to us!"

But Greaves was unmoved. He continued appearing as though in a trance. "There are others out there. *Friends.* They will come to our aid. But we must be ready...and we must ask them for help...!"

J ULY 1947...

Strange sheets of thin, burning metal coated the desert hillside. US Army personnel roamed about the area and a giant, silver disc was burrowed into the desert. A rancher had discovered the wreckage and called the authorities who, unlike in 1941, were better prepared to respond and contain the crash site. Tall, gray bodies had been discovered. One of them, just like the Cape Girardeau crash, was alive. These gray aliens were different than the ones discovered in Cape Girardeau, though. They were tall and slender whereas Bandit and his kind were short and stocky. The country was still celebrating its victory in the Second World War. Everyone was ready to move into peace. But, threats remained. For many in Washington, they were transfixed on the Soviet threat. For the slightly older and wiser Patrick Greaves, he knew the real threat came from above.

Greaves had been fired from the FBI after he recovered from his ordeal at Peenemunde. Hoover believed that Greaves had been compromised by the Nazis. General Donovan of the OSS did not agree with Hoover's assessment. After Hoover canned Greaves, Donovan hired Greaves to be a full-time OSS man. After the war had ended, the OSS was folded into the newly formed Central Intelligence Agency. Greaves was then tasked with ensuring that the atomic secrets of the US military were protected. That was why he was assigned to the US Army base in Roswell, New Mexico, where the 509th Composite Group was located. This was the group that dropped the two atomic bombs on Japan that ended the Pacific Theater of the Second World War.

Now, here Greaves was, standing over another alien wreck. Something in the back of his mind told him that the warning that Bandit and the other alien had imparted to him to give to FDR back in 1945 was coming true: more aliens were coming. This was but the first wave. But he was not filled with fear or consternation. Instead, Greaves was hopeful. Now they had access yet again to sophisticated alien technology that they might be able to build their own defenses from. Now they could prepare—and possibly ask—for help from other, more advanced aliens.

Greaves lit a cigarette and smiled. *We're back in business!* He thought excitedly to himself, sensing excitement and the prospects of an entirely new adventure ahead. Now, he just had to cover this incident up and alert his leaders in Washington.

J ULY 17, 1952, 9:52 PM EASTERN TIME...

President Harry S. Truman gritted his teeth as more reports of strange sightings over the Washington night sky occurred. Were they under attack? Was someone trying to contact them? He stood in the Oval Office, pacing, with the phone pressed to his ear. Truman's Air Force aide, Lieutenant Gerald "Grudge" Donovan sat in the chair on the right side of the famous Resolute desk, dutifully jotting notes on a yellow legal pad while he had another handset placed near his left ear, his left hand covering the receiver, so the person at the other end wouldn't hear.

Donovan could tell that the thirty-third American president was angry. This was the second weekend in a row where dozens of unknown craft had basically harassed the nation's capital, buzzing Andrews Air Force Base in nearby Maryland, Washington National Airport, Capitol Hill, and even the White House itself. The previous weekend, Secret Service had forced Truman into the bunker below the White House. This weekend, Truman had staked his position out in the Oval Office and he refused to leave. That summer in 1952, the whole country had been gripped by "UFO fever" in Truman's words.

"So are these them?" Truman asked in a frustrated tone. The country had not been on this high of an alert level since the Second World War.

"Yes, Mr. President." The voice of the officer at Wright-Patterson Air Force Base in Ohio responded.

Truman shook his head. Back in 1947, an alien craft had crash-landed in the desert of Roswell, New Mexico. But that was only the beginning. After recovering the craft the military had captured one of the craft's pilots, a gray alien, and had him currently in containment at Wright-Patterson. The alien was friendly—as friendly as a being from another world with working knowledge of advanced technology and the universe could be. Truman had briefly met the strange being in Roswell back in 1947. Over the years, several more spacecraft had been captured in the United States.

Truman had categorically denied the alien's request to transmit a message back to his home-world, for fear that more of his kind would come. The president was not from behind the mountain, as his mother would say. He knew an invasion force when he saw one. Truman needed some buy-in from their visitor before just opening the castle gate and encouraging more to come. The alien in their custody, though, had warned them that failure to send notice to his people would only bring more to Earth. Apparently, like the Americans, the aliens rarely left their own behind.

"Do your people suspect this to be a prelude to an attack?" Truman asked, glancing out the window of the Oval Office, as if reflexively trying to visualize one of the dozens of glowing orbs that was plaguing radar operators at Washington National Airport and Andrews, as well as pilots aboard civilian airliners and the F-94 Starfire fighter jets that had been deployed from nearby Delaware to form a combat air patrol over Washington.

"Sir, I think they're trying to get your attention." The officer on the other end said cryptically.

Truman and Donovan exchanged bewildered glances. "Well, General, they've got it!" The president whooped.

Donovan stood. "Mr. President, I think what the general is saying is that these things want to talk to you..."

Truman's eyes widened. He had, after all, met Stalin who was far scarier to the former haberdasher from Independence, Missouri than some tiny gray people were. Then again, though, Stalin's forces weren't currently buzzing the White House on a balmy summer evening. "How could they even know who I am?" Truman inquired.

"Sir, they monitor all of our radio communications." The general on the other line said.

"They've never tried contacting us this way before." Truman responded skeptically.

"Well, Mr. President, earlier this evening there was a breach here at the base." The general said ominously.

Truman looked confused. "What-what kind of breach?"

"Involving the gray." The general began to explain.

Truman was annoyed. The whole sky was falling down upon the nation's capital and the general was talking about a security breach at his base in Ohio. "And?" Truman prompted angrily.

"One of our scientists here—a young Brit—" The general began.

Donovan waved over at Truman to get his attention. Still covering the receiver with his left hand, Donovan whispered, "Dr. Lee Chilton!"

Truman was even more confused. "Who?" He thundered over the line and at his Air Force adjutant.

"Lee Chilton, a preeminent nuclear physicist—one of the youngest in the world—handpicked by Vannevar Bush to run studies on the alien craft. He's from Liverpool, sir." The general explained, sounding annoyed that the junior officer was interrupting him.

Truman blinked, vaguely remembering the scrawny British scientist he had met a few years ago. "Oh, but he was a kid!" Truman quipped, remembering that Chilton was a whiz kid who had received his first Ph.D. in physics at the age of 17. "What does he have to do with this?" Truman demanded to know.

"Someone let the Visitor—" That was one of the nicknames the Americans had for the gray. The other was friend." The general continued, "—out of his holding area and gain access to one of the visitor's communications systems." The general said.

Truman was mortified. He had expressly forbidden direct contact between the Americans and whatever government represented the gray. "Was he under some kind of...you know...mind control, this Dr. Chilton?" Truman asked, unable to fathom why anyone would willingly help the alien. After all, Truman feared that the human race would become much like the old Aztecs upon discovery by the Spanish Conquistadores: their cities destroyed and their people were enslaved in short order after contact with the more advanced race.

"Sir, Dr. Chilton has confessed to the MPs here. He claims that he needed assistance on his current research project and the gray informed him that the problem needed inputs from his people off-world." The general explained in his typical brusque military tone.

Truman was shocked. The entire national security of the United States upended by a teenager! "Good heavens!" He said exasperatedly at the thought. "He just picked up the phone and called our friends?!"

Donovan nodded.

"Basically, yes, sir." The general said in an equally mystified tone.

"H-How do I meet these things?" Truman asked. "I mean, will they land on the front lawn here tonight...?"

"Sir, Dr. Chilton and our friend insist they can make contact with the squadron over Washington and direct them to land here." The general said.

Truman shook his head. "Well, then, general, put on your Sunday's best...because it looks like we'll be having an interstellar peace conference!"

When Truman hung up the phone, he looked over at Lieutenant Donovan who was in shock. Their entire strategy for dealing with the aliens—avoidance and collection of any technology—had just been upended. Donovan had been with the Majestic-12 program for the last couple of years, serving as the project's liaison to President Truman. He had known Dr. Chilton during that time and found the young man to be utterly brilliant and wholly loathsome. It did not surprise Donovan at all that Chilton would defy a presidential directive in order to have his question answered by the aliens.

Truman leaned on the Resolute desk, deep in contemplation. They had only just gotten used to the terrible rhythm of the Cold War after having escaped the killing fields of the Second World War. Now, in the last six months of his presidency, Truman was having to initiate an entirely new form of diplomacy—with beings from another planet.

What's more, Truman had no plan for action on this one. He was making things up now on the fly. There was a certain degree of comfort in knowing that Truman was, yet again, blazing a new trail that would set the course of the next century of America's development. Then again, though, Truman was mortified that one wrong move could lead to the extinction of the human race. The last eight years of his life as president had been truly momentous for a man who was, not long ago, bankrupt and considered to be "barely literate" by his critics.

Donovan was on the phone still, though he had switched over from the general at Wright-Patterson to another officer who had been tracking the craft over the capital. "Mr. President, radar tracks indicate the vehicles are moving away from Washington—at more than 7,000 miles per hour!"

Truman shook his head, still mulling over what he had to do next. "How could Wright-Pat have gotten the message to them so fast?" Truman inquired, furrowing his brow in the process.

"It's like the general said, sir, our friends monitor all radio traffic—civilian and military alike. They probably heard our chatter about the gray and know we're responding to them the way they wanted us to respond." Donovan speculated, though he spoke with a degree of confidence that sent a chill down Truman's pine.

What Truman heard was that there was an advanced group of beings penetrating American airspace at will, harassing US military installations, listening in to all manner of communications—with the ability to totally obliterate the country—now forcing the American president to respond in ways they desired. This was not the way a superpower behaved, in Truman's estimation. Despite his concerns, though, Truman was more miffed at the young scientist who had willingly put the country— the whole planet—in this predicament. "I need to know about this Dr. Chilton." Truman said sternly.

Donovan smirked at the thought of the scientist. "You mean, Boy Wonder, sir?"

Truman looked up with concern.

A sheepish look befell Donovan's face. "Sorry, Mr. President, but the kid is insufferable even on a good day."

"You know him well?" Truman prodded.

Donovan hung up the phone as the final report was placed. "The craft are dispersing."

Truman nodded. "But you know this Dr. Chilton well?"

Donovan shook his head. "One doesn't really know Dr. Chilton, sir. One is made to listen to him share his opinion on everything from science to nutrition and if one disagrees, one is berated endlessly for it."

Truman glowered. "A real grandstander, eh?"

Donovan nodded. "It wouldn't be half so bad if he took our protocols seriously. But the only thing he takes seriously is his own work and everyone else can go to hell, in his mind."

Truman shook his head. "Sounds like a bit of a knucklehead."

"That's one way of putting it, sir. But he was Vannevar Bush's top pick for the program that you formed after Roswell. Most of our advances over the last five years have been because of his research." Donovan admitted with a hint of bitterness in his voice.

"Truman could detect the bitterness. "But you don't care much for him?"

Donovan glanced toward the phone that Truman had hung up. "Sir, by the end of this weekend, he may have just ended human existence as we know it."

Feeling some relief as the evening's craziness was coming to an end, Truman sighed. He shook his head. "Son, they tell me I could end the world at a moment's notice."

Donovan nodded.

"Should I order Dr. Chilton be removed from Majestic?" Truman asked, looking at Donovan's facial expressions for a cue as what to do next. "He's already proven himself a security risk..." Truman trailed, hoping to elicit a response from Donovan.

Donovan stiffened as he realized the president was looking to him for an answer. He despised Chilton more than anyone he had met in government service. Yet, Donovan meant what he had said: Chilton was the best mind, outside of the old scientists who had helped build the atomic bomb and develop Majestic-12 in 1947, and who were mostly dying off today. "Sir, he violated our defense protocols that you laid down back in '47." Donovan said in a neutral tone, his face betraying that neutrality.

Truman smirked. "That's not what I asked, Lieutenant."

Donovan looked away and then back at Truman. "Mr. President, Lee is an egoist. He is a genius. He is irrational. He is young. But he just may be the only man standing between this country—the world—and some kind of alien invasion."

"Truman took in Donovan's words. There was a reason he had come to trust the young adjutant over his older advisers on these matters. He was painfully fair—even when it clearly would have benefited him to have Chilton removed from MJ-12. He remained silent for a moment, incensed that this young Brit had put America in such a dangerous position tonight.

"We need him." Donovan affirmed.

Truman raised his hand, motioning for Lieutenant Donovan to stop. Truman had made up his mind. "Chilton will remain, then. And I will meet these things and begin an official dialog." Truman shook his head. "I really wanted to avoid this." He said with regret in his voice. "Meeting the Conquistadores didn't do Montezuma any favors in the end, did it?" Truman mused aloud.

Donovan shrugged. "Well, sir, Montezuma wasn't some innocent. He was bathed in blood by the time that Cortes and the Conquistadores met with him..."

Truman frowned. "And I'm not, Lieutenant?"

Donovan grimaced at the mention of the nuclear bombs being dropped on Hiroshima and Nagasaki. "That's different, sir. Your decision saved many more lives than it killed."

Truman nodded and looked out at the night sky above the White House, through the huge windows in the back of the Oval Office. He sighed. "Montezuma thought all of those human sacrifices would protect his people from their god's vengeance."

"Donovan glowered. "Sir..."

Truman smiled ruefully as he stared out at the night sky above them, disbelieving that the historic skies above Washington had become something of an unknown expanse. "I've never regretted dropping those bombs, Mr. Donovan." He explained. "Not once." Truman reaffirmed. "I'll have to answer to God for that choice. But I've made my peace with it long ago." He continued. "Will they be as forgiving as I believe my God will be, though?" Truman asked rhetorically. "Will they understand any more than Cortes and his Conquistadores understood Montezuma when they saw the tens of thousands of sacrifices?"

Donovan looked away. "Cortes and his lot were out for Aztec gold, sir. All of the understanding in the world wouldn't have stopped them from destroying that civilization."

Truman shrugged. "Maybe our friends are out for something like that from us, too...and maybe they're just as willing to knock us out of the way. Just like Cortes was willing to take the Aztecs out."

Donovan walked up behind the president. "Sir, it's best not to dwell on these thoughts."

Truman shot his military aide an angry glance. "I'm the president, Mr. Donovan. If I don't think these thoughts, who will?" Truman looked back upon the night sky just beyond the palatial windows of the Oval Office. The great white jail. That was how Truman had famously described the White House a few years back. He felt the same locked away in the White House on this momentous night, the weight of the world yet again pressing down upon him.

"In six months' time I'll be out of this glorified prison, Mr. Donovan. And until tonight, despite what Ike and his Republican attack dogs said of me during the campaign this year, I genuinely thought I'd be leaving the country in better shape than when I had found it." Truman said sadly. "Now I really don't quite know..."

Donovan recoiled, concerned that his president's mental health was in a bad way. "Mr. President, you're about to make history. You're about to make an alliance with another world." He said, his concerns about security melding with his excitement of the unknown—a sense of wonder filling him that had initially compelled him to become a fighter pilot.

Truman smiled. "That's exactly what Montezuma thought when he first came across Cortes and the Conquistadores." He said in a sheepish tone. "One way or the other, I suppose I'm just destined to make history."

Donovan nodded. "Yes, sir."

Truman nodded. "And so I will. For better or worse.